Fanny Burney

The Wanderer
Volume 5

Fanny Burney

The Wanderer
Volume 5

1st Edition | ISBN: 978-3-75232-989-6

Place of Publication: Frankfurt am Main, Germany

Year of Publication: 2020

Outlook Verlag GmbH, Germany.

Reproduction of the original.

THE WANDERER

By Fanny Burney
Vol V

CHAPTER LXXVII

The final purposes for which man is ordained to move in this nether sphere, will for ever remain disputable, while the doubts to which it gives rise can be answered only by fellow-doubters: but that the basis of his social comfort is confidence, is an axiom that waits no revelation, requires no logic, and dispenses with mathematical accuracy for proof: it is an axiom that comes home, straight forward and intuitively, to our 'business and bosoms;'—there, with life, to lodge.

Juliet, therefore, in this rustic abode, surrounded by the clinging affection of instinctive partiality, felt a sense of security, more potent in its simplicity, than she could have owed to any engagement, even of honour, even of law, even of duty. And, while to the fond mother and her little ones, she was every moment newly endeared, she experienced herself, in their favour, an increase of regard, that excited in her an ardent desire to make this her permanent dwelling, till she could procure tidings from Gabriella.

The night-scene, nevertheless, hung upon her with perplexity. The good dame never reverted to it, evidently not imagining that it had been observed; and persuaded that the entrance, at that moment, of her guest, had been accidental. She constantly evaded to speak of her husband, or of his affairs; while all her happiness, and almost her very existence, seemed wrapt up in her children.

Unable to devise any better method of arriving at the subject, Juliet, at length, determined upon relating the story of the hut. She watched for an opportunity, when the little boy and girl, whom she would not risk frightening, were asleep; and then, while occupied at her needle, began detailing every circumstance of that affair.

The narrative of the place, and of the family, sufficed to draw, at once, from the dame the exclamation, 'O, you been gone, then, to Nat Mixon's? That be just he; and her, too. They be none o' the koindest, that be sure, poor folk!'

But at the history of the calling up in the night; the rising, passing, and precautions; the dame changed colour, and, with palpable disturbance, enquired upon what day of the week this had happened: she revived, however, upon being answered that it was Thursday, simply saying, 'Mercy be proised! that be a day as can do me no harm.'

But, at the description of the sack, the lumpish sound, and the subsequent appearance of a clot of blood, the poor woman turned pale; and, blessing herself, said, 'The La be good unto me! Nat Mixon wull be paid, at last, for all his bad ways! for, sure and sure, the devil do owe un a grudge, or a would no ha' let a straunger in, to bear eye sight to's goings on! 'T be a mercy 't be no worse, for an if 't had bin a Friday—'

She checked herself, but looked much troubled. Juliet, affrighted by her own conjectures, would have stopt; the dame, however, begged her to go on: but when she mentioned the cupboard, and the door smeared with blood, the poor woman, unable to contain her feelings, caught her guest by the arm, and exclaimed, 'You wull no' inform against un, wull you?'

'Indeed, I should be most reluctant,' answered Juliet, 'to inform against people who, be they what they may, admitted me to a night's lodging, when I was in distress: nevertheless—what am I to think of these appearances? Meetings in the dead of the night, so dark, private, and clandestine?'

'But, who could 't be as did call up Nat?' interrupted Dame Fairfield; 'for my husband do go only o' the Friday.—' and then, giving a loud scream, 'La be good unto me!' she continued, 'if an't be last month, 't be my husband for sure! for a could no' go o' the Friday, being the great fair!'

The expression of horrour now depicted upon the countenance of Juliet, told the dame the mischief done by her unguarded speech; and, in a panic uncontroulable, she flung her apron over her face, and sobbed out, ''T be all blown, then, and we, we be all no better than ondone!'

Shocked, grieved, and appalled at this detection, and uncertain whither it might lead, or what might be its extent, the thoughts of Juliet were now all engrossed in considering how immediately to abscond from a situation so alarming and perilous.

In a few minutes, Dame Fairfield, starting up, ran precipitately to the bed, calling out, 'Come, my pretty ones, come, my dearys! come and down o' your knees to the good gentlewoman, and praoy her to ha' mercy o' poor daddy; for if so be a come to be honged and transported, you can never show your poor innocent pretty faces agen! Come, little dearys, come! down o' your marrow-bones; and praoy her to be so good as not to be hard-hearted; for if a do be so onkoind as to inform against us, we be all ondone!'

Juliet would have stopt this scene, but it was not possible; the children, though comprehending nothing that was said, and crying at being awaked, obeyed; and, falling at her feet, and supporting themselves by her gown, said, 'Pay, dood ady, don't hurt daddy! pay don't, dood ady!'

Touched, yet filled with augmented dismay by their prayers, Juliet, tenderly embracing, carried them back to bed; and, with words of comfort, and kind promises, soon hushed them again to sleep.

But the mother was not to be appeased; she had flung herself upon her knees, and upon her knees she pertinaciously kept; sobbing as if her heart were bursting, and lamenting that her husband never would listen to her, or things would not have come to such a pass.

Juliet, full of compassion, yet shuddering, attempted to console her, but would enter into no engagement. Pity, in such a case, however sincerely felt, could not take the lead; humanity itself invoked justice; and she determined to let no personal consideration whatsoever, interfere any longer with her causing an immediate investigation to be made into this fearful business.

The poor woman would not quit the floor, even when, in despondence, she gave over her kneeling importunity. Juliet, from the instant that she discovered how deeply the husband was involved, forbore all enquiry that might make the wife an informer against him; and sate by her side, trying to revive her, with offers of friendship and assistance.

But when, anxious to escape from this eventful Forest, and still confiding in the simplicity and goodness of her hostess, she begged a clear direction to the shortest way for getting to the high road; saying, 'Alas! how little had I imagined that there had been any spot in England, where travellers were thus dreadfully waylaid to their destruction!' Dame Fairfield, suddenly ceasing her outcries, demanded what she meant; saying, 'Why sure, and sure, there be no daunger to nobody in our Forest! We do go up it and down it, noight and day, without no manner of fear; and though I do come from afar off myself, being but a straunger in these parts, till I was married; my feather-in-law, who has lived in them, mon and boy, better than ninety and odd years,—for, thof a be still as fresh as a rose, a be a'most a hondred; he do tell me that a would carry his gold watch, if a had one, in his open hand, from top to bottom of our nine walks, in the pitch of the night; and a should aunswer to come to no harm; for a had never heard of a traveller as had had so much as a hair of his head hurt in the New Forest.'

'What is it you tell me, my good dame?' cried Juliet amazed: 'What are these alarming scenes that I have witnessed? And why are your apprehensions for your husband so direful?'

'The La be good unto me!' exclaimed the dame: 'why sure and sure you do no' go to think the poor mon be a murderer?'

'I am disposed to think whatever you will bid me,' replied Juliet, 'for I see in you such perfect truth and candour, that I cannot hesitate in giving you my belief.'

'Why the La be good unto me, my good gentlewoman, there be but small need to make bad worse! What the poor mon ha' done, may bring un to be

4

honged and transported; but if so be a had killed a mon, a might go to old Nick besoides; and no one could say a deserved ony better.'

Juliet earnestly begged an explanation; and Dame Fairfield then confessed, that her husband and Nat Mixon were deer-stealers.

After the tremendous sensations to which the mistake of Juliet, from her ignorance of this species of traffic, had given rise, so unexpected a solution of her perplexity, made this crime, contrasted with the assassination of a fellow-creature, appear venial. But though relieved from personal terrours, she would not hazard weakening the morality, in lessening the fears of the good, but uncultivated Dame Fairfield, by making her participate in the comparative view taken by herself, of the greater with the less offence. She represented, therefore, warmly and clearly, the turpitude of all failure of probity; dwelling most especially upon the heinousness of a breach of trust.

The good woman readily said, that she knew, well enough, that the deer were as much the King's Majesty's as the Forest; and that she had told it over and over to her husband; and bid him prepare for his latter end, if he would follow such courses: 'But the main bleame, it do all lie in Nat Mixon; for a be as bad a mon as a body might wish to set eyes on. And a does always say a likes ony thing better than work. It be he has led my poor husband astray: for, thof a be but a bad mon, at best, to my mishap! a was a good sort of a husband enough, poor mon, till a took to these courses. But a knows I do no' like un for that; and that makes it, that a does no' much like me. But I would no' ha' un come to be honged or transported, if so be a was as onkoind agen! I would sooner go with un to prison; thof it be but a dismal life to be shut up by dark walls, and iron bars for to see out of! but I'd do it for sure and sure, not to forsake un, poor mon! in his need; if so be I could get wherewithal to keep my little dearys.'

Touched by such genuine and virtuous simplicity, Juliet now promised to apply to some powerful gentleman, to take her husband from the temptation of his present situation; and to settle them all at a distance from the Forest.

The good woman, at this idea, started up in an extacy, and jumped about the room, to give some vent to her joy; kissing her little ones till she nearly suffocated them; and telling them, for sure and certain, that they had gotten an angel come amongst them, to save them all from shame. 'For now,' she continued, 'if we do but get un away from Nat Mixon and his wife, who be the worst mon in all the Forest, a wull think no more of selling unlawful goods than unlawful geame.'

Juliet, though delighted at her happiness, was struck with the words 'unlawful goods;' which she involuntarily repeated. Dame Fairfield, unable, at this moment, to practise any restraint upon her feelings, plumply, then, acknowledged that Nat Mixon was a smuggler, as well as a deer-stealer: and that three of them were gone, even now, about the country, selling laces, and cambrics, and gloves, just brought to land.

This additional misdemeanour, considerably abated the hopes of reformation which had been conceived by Juliet; and every word that, inadvertently, escaped from the unguarded dame, brought conviction that the man was thoroughly worthless. To give him, nevertheless, if possible, the means to amend; and, at all events, to succour his good wife, and lovely children, occupied as much of the thoughts of Juliet as could be drawn, by humanity, from the danger of her own situation, and her solicitude to escape from the Forest.

More fearful than ever of losing her way, and falling into new evil, she again entreated Dame Fairfield to accompany her to the next town on the morrow. The dame agreed to every thing; and then, light of heart, though heavy with fatigue, went to rest; and was instantly visited by the best physician to all our cares.

Juliet, also, courted repose; and not utterly in vain; though it came not to the relief of her anxious spirits, agitated by all the anticipating inquietude of foresight, with the same salutary facility with which it instantly hushed the fears and the griefs of the unreflecting, though feeling Dame Fairfield.

The moment that the babbling little voices of the children reached, the next morning, the ear of Juliet, she descended from her small chamber, to hasten the breakfast, and to quicken her departure. Dame Fairfield, during the preparations and the repast, happy in new hope, and solaced by unburthening her heart, conversed, without reserve, upon her affairs; and the picture which her ingenuous avowals, and simple details, offered to the mental view of Juliet, presented to her a new sight of human life; but a sight from which she turned with equal sadness and amazement.

The wretched man of the hut, of whom the poor dame's husband was the servile accomplice, was the leader in all the illicit adventures of the New Forest. Another cottager, also, was entirely under his direction; though the difficulty and danger attendant upon their principal traffic, great search being always made after a lost deer, caused it to be rarely repeated; but smaller game; hares, pheasants, and partridges, were easily inveigled, by an adroit dispersion of grain, to a place proper for their seizure; and it required not much skill to frame stories for satisfying purchasers, who were generally too eager for possession, to be scrupulous in investigating the means by which their luxury was so cheaply indulged.

The fixed day of rendezvous was every Friday month, that each might be ready for his part of the enterprize.

Juliet, the dame imagined, had been admitted because it was Thursday, and that her husband had not given notice that he should change his day, on account of the fair; besides which, neither Mixon, she said, nor his wife, ever refused money, be it ever so dangerous. He and his family nearly subsisted upon the game which could not be got off in time; or the refuse; or parts that were too suspicious for sale, of the deer. But Dame Fairfield, though at the expence of the most terrible quarrels, and even ill usage from her husband, never would consent to touch, nor suffer her children to eat, what was not their own; 'for I do tell un,' she continued, 'it might strangle us down our throats; for it be all his King's Majesty's; and I do no' know why we should take hisn goods, when a do never come to take none of ours! for we be never mislested, night nor day. And a do deserve well of us all; for a be as good a gentlemon as ever broke bread! which we did all see, when a was in these parts; as well as his good lady, the Queen, who had a smile for the lowest of us, God bless un! and all their pretty ones! for they were made up of good nature and charity; and had no more pride than the new-born baby. And we did all love 'em, when they were in these parts, so as the like never was seen before.'

With regard to the smuggling, there were three men, she said, who came over, alternately, from beyond seas, with counterband merchandize. They landed where they could, and, if they were surprised, they knew how to hide their goods, and pass for poor fishermen, blown over by foul winds: for they had always fishing tackle ready to shew. They had agents all round the coast, prepared to deal with them; but when they came to the Forest, they always treated with Mixon.

Her friend near the turnpike, at Salisbury, commonly kept a good store of articles; which she carried about, occasionally, to the ladies of the town. 'And I ha' had sums and sums of goods,' she added, 'here, oftentimes, myself; and then I do no dare to leave the house for one yearthly moment; for we be all no better than slaves when the smugglers be here, for fear of some informer. And I do tell my poor husband, we should be mainly happier to work our hands to the bone, ony day of the year, so we did but live by the King's Majesty's laws, than to make money by being always in a quandary. And a might see the truth of what I do say, if a would no' blind his poor eyes; or Nat Mixon, thof a do get a power of money, do live the most pitiful of us all, for the fear of being found out: a does no' dare get un a hat, nor a waistcoat like to another mon. And his wife be the dirtiest beast in all the Forest. And their house and garden be no better than a piggery. So that they've no joy of life. They be but bad people at best, poor folk! And Nat be main cross-grained; for, with all his care, a do look to be took up every blessed day; and that don't much mend a mon's humour.'

Ah, thought Juliet, were the wilful, but unreflecting purchaser, amenable to sharing the public punishment of the tempted and needy instrument,—how soon would this traffic die away; and every country live by its own means; or by its own fair commerce!

They had all, the dame said, been hard at work, to cover some goods under ground, the very night of Juliet's arrival: and they had put what was for immediate sale into hods, spread over with potatoes, to convey to different places. When Juliet had tapped at the door, the dame had concluded it to be her husband, returned for something that had been forgotten; but the sight of a stranger, she said, though it were but a woman, made her think that they were all undone; for the changed dress of Juliet impeded any recollection of her, till she spoke.

In the communication to which this discourse gave rise, Juliet, with surprize, and even with consternation, learnt, how pernicious were the ravages of dishonest cupidity; how subversive alike of fair prosperity, and genial happiness, even in the bosom of retired and beautiful rusticity. For those who were employed in poaching, purloining wood, or concealing illicit merchandize by night, were as incapable of the arts and vigour of industry by day, as they were torpid to the charms and animation of the surrounding beauties of nature. Their severest labour received no pay, but from fearful, accidental, and perilous dexterity; their best success was blighted by constant apprehension of detection. Reproachful with each other, suspicious of their neighbours, and gloomy in themselves, they were still greater strangers to civilized manners than to social morality.

In the midst, however, of the dejection excited by such a view of human frailty, Juliet, whose heart always panted to love, and prided in esteeming her fellow-creatures, had the consolation to gather, that the houses which contained these unworthy members of the community were few, in comparison with those which were inhabited by persons of unsullied probity; that several of the cottagers were even exemplary for assiduous laboriousness and good conduct; and that many of the farmers and their families were universally respected.

CHAPTER LXXVIII

When Dame Fairfield was nearly ready, Juliet, to forward the march, set out with the two children; but had scarcely quitted the house, when the sight of a man, advancing towards the habitation, made her plant herself behind a tree, to examine him before she ventured to proceed.

She observed that he stopt, every two or three minutes, himself, to take an inquisitive view all around him; frequently bending upon the ground, and appearing to be upon some eager search.

As he approached, she thought that his air was familiar to her; she regarded him more earnestly as he drew nearer; what, then, was her horrour to recognize the pilot!

She glided back, instantaneously, to the house, beckoning to the children to follow; and, rushing upon Dame Fairfield, and, taking both her hands, she faintly ejaculated, 'Oh my good dame!—hide, conceal me, I entreat!—I am pursued by a cruel enemy, and lost if you are not my friend!—Serve, save me, now, and I will be yours to the end of my life!'

'That I wull!' answered the dame, delighted; 'if you wull but be so koind as to save my poor husband the sheame of being honged or transported, I wull go through fire and water to serve you, to the longest day I have to live upon the feace of God's yearth!'

Then, making the children play without doors, that they might not observe what passed, she told Juliet to bolt herself into the upper chamber.

In a few minutes, the children, running into the house, called out, 'Mam, mam, yonder be dad!'

The dame went forth to meet him; and Juliet spent nearly half an hour in the most cruel suspense.

Dame Fairfield then came to her; and, by the discourse that ensued, she found that the pilot was one of the smugglers who brought merchandize to Mixon; and heard that he and Fairfield had thus unexpectedly returned, in search of a piece of fine broad French lace, of great value, which was missing; and which Fairfield suspected to have dropt from one of his parcels, while he was making his assortments, by the light of the lanthorn. She had been, she said, helping them to look for it, high and low; but had stolen away, for an instant, to bring this account; and to beg Juliet not to be frightened, because though, if Fairfield would go up stairs, she could not hinder him, she would take care that the smuggler should not follow.

Juliet was now seized with a panic that nearly bereft her of all hope; and Dame Fairfield was so much touched by the sight of her sufferings, that she descended, unbidden, to endeavour to discover some means to facilitate an escape.

That the pilot should prove to be a smuggler, caused no surprize to Juliet; but that accident should so cruelly be her foe, as to lead her to the spot where he deposited and negociated his merchandize, at the very period when his affairs brought him thither himself; that she should find her chosen retreat her bane; and that, even where she was unpursued, she should be overtaken; was a stroke of misfortune as severe as it was unexpected.

And, soon after, she found her situation still more terrible than she had imagined it. Fairfield, presently entering the kitchen, to take some food, accused his wife, in a loud and angry tone, of having abetted an imposter. Mounseer, the smuggler, he said, had not come to these parts, this time, merely for his own private business. He had been offered a great reward for discovering a young gentlewoman who had run away; and who turned out to be no other than the very same that she had been such a ninny as to impose upon Dame Goss, at Salisbury; and who had made off without paying for her board and lodging.

The dame warmly declared, that this could not be possible; that it must be some other gentlewoman; for that a person who could be so kind to her children could not have so black a heart.

Fairfield, with bitter reproaches against her folly, persisted in the accusation: stating, that, upon Dame Goss's going to the post-office for a letter, it had been refused to her, because of its being directed to a person advertised in the public news-papers; and Dame Goss had been sent back, with an excuse, to while away the time, till somebody should follow, to confront the gentlewoman with the advertisement. But Dame Goss, instead of keeping a sharp watch, had been over-persuaded to go of an errand; and she had no sooner turned her back, than the gentlewoman made off. However, they had written to the news-papers that she was somewhere in those parts; and they could do no more; for there was no right to seize her; for the advertisement only desired to know where she might be heard of, and found. It had made a rare hue and cry in the town; and Mounseer, the smuggler, who had come down to Salisbury along with another outlandish man, had traced the gentlewoman as far as to Romsey; but could not find out what had become of her afterwards. The other outlandish man, who was as rich as a Duke, and was to pay the reward, had stopt at Salisbury, for tidings: upon which Mounseer, the smuggler, thought he might as well come on, and see a bit after his own business by the way; for it would not lose much time; and he might not get to these parts again for months.

The silence that ensued, gave Juliet an afflicting presentiment that she had lost, by this history, her friend and advocate: and accordingly, when, upon her husband's returning to his search, the dame re-mounted the stairs, her air was so changed, that Juliet, again clasping her hands, cried, 'Oh! Dame Fairfield! —Kind, good Dame Fairfield! judge me not till you know me better! Aid me still, my good dame, in pity, in charity aid me!—for, believe me, I am innocent!'

'Why then so I wull!' cried the dame, resuming her looks of mild good will; 'I wull believe you! And I'll holp you too, for sure: for now you be under my own poor roof, 'twould be like unto a false heart to give you up to your enemies. Besoides, I do think in my conscience you wull pay every one his own, when you've got wherewithal. And it be but hard to expect it before. And I do say, that a person that could be so koind to my little Jacky and Jenny, in their need, must have a good heart of her own; and would no' wrong no yearthly creature, unless a could no' holp it.'

She then promised to watch the moment of the smuggler's turning round to the garden-side of the house, to assist her flight; and, once a few yards distant, all would be safe; for her change of clothes from what she had worn at Salisbury, would secure her from any body's recollection.

This, in a few minutes, was performed; and, without daring to see the children, who would have cried at her departure, Juliet took a hasty leave, silent but full of gratitude, of the good dame; into whose bosom, as her hand refused it, she slipt a guinea for the little ones; and, having received full directions, set forward, by the shortest cut, to the nearest high road.

She reached it unannoyed, but breathless; and seated herself upon a bank by its side; not to hesitate which way to turn; the right and the left were alike unknown to her, and alike liable to danger; but to recover respiration, and force to proceed.

She could now form no plan, save to hasten to some other part of the country; certain that here she was sought all around; and conscious that the disguise of her habiliment, if not already betrayed, must shortly, from a thousand accidents, prove nugatory.

In her ignorance what course the pilot might take, upon quitting the cottage of Fairfield, she determined upon seeking, immediately, some decent lodging for the rest of the day; hoping thus, should he pursue the same route, to escape being overtaken.

She had soon the satisfaction to come to a small habitation, a little out of the high road, where she was accommodated, by a man and his wife, with a room that precisely answered her purpose: and here she spent the night.

Thankful in obtaining any sort of tranquillity, she would fain have remained longer; but she durst not continue in the neighbourhood of Fairfield; and, the following morning, she re-commenced her wanderings.

She asked the way to Salisbury, though merely that she might take an opposite direction. She ventured not to raise her eyes from the earth, nor to cast even a glance at any one whom she passed. She held her handkerchief to her face at the sound of every carriage; and trembled at the approach of every horseman. Her steps were quick and eager; though not more precipitate to fly from those by whom she was followed, than fearful of being observed by those whom she met.

In a short time, the sight of several hostlers, helpers, and postilions, before a large house, which appeared to be a capital inn, made her cross the way. She wished to turn wholly from the high road; but low brick-walls had now, on either side, taken place of hedges, and she searched in vain for an opening. Her earnestness to press onward, joined to her fear of looking up, made her soon follow, unconsciously, an ordinary man, till she was so close behind him, as suddenly to perceive, by his now well known coat, that he was the pilot! A scream struggled to escape her, in the surprize of her affright; but she stifled it, and, turning short back, speeded her retrograde way with all her force.

She had reason, however, to fear that her uncontrollable first emotion had caught his notice, for she heard footsteps following. Hopeless of saving herself, if watched or suspected, by flight; as she knew that there was no turning for at least half a mile; she darted precipitately into the inn; which seemed alone to offer her even a shadow of any chance of concealment. She rushed past ostlers, helpers, postilions, and waiters; seized the hand of the first female that she met; and hastily begged to be shewn to a room.

The chambermaid, astonished at such a request from a person no better equipped, pertly asked what she meant.

Juliet, whose apprehensive eyes roved everywhere, now saw the pilot at the door.

She held the maid by the arm, and, in a voice scarcely audible, entreated to be taken any where that she might be alone; and had the presence of mind to hint at a recompence.

This instantly prevailed. The maid said, 'Well, come along!' and led her to a small apartment up stairs.

Juliet put a shilling into her hand, and was then left to herself.

In an agony of suffering that disordered her whole frame, What a life, she cried, is this that I lead! How tremendous, and how degrading! Is it possible that even what I fly can be more dreadful?

This question restored her fortitude. Ah yes! ah yes! she cried, all passing evil is preferable to such a termination!

She now composed her spirits, and, while deliberating how she might make a friend of the maid, to aid her escape, perceived, from the window, the pilot, in a stable-yard, examining a horse, for which he seemed to be bartering.

This determined her to attempt to regain the cottage which she had last quitted, and thence to try some opposite route.

Swiftly she descended the stairs; a general bustle from some new arrival enabled her to pass unnoticed; but a chaise was at the door, and she was forced to make way for a gentleman, who had just quitted it, to enter the house. Unavoidably, by this movement, she saw the gentleman also; the colour instantly forsook her cheeks and lips; her feet tottered, and she fell.

She was immediately surrounded by waiters; but the gentleman, who, observing only her dress, concluded her to belong to the house, walked on into the kitchen, and asked, in broken English, for the landlord or landlady.

Juliet, whose fall had been the effect of a sudden deprivation of strength, from an abrupt sensation of horrour, had not fainted. She heard, therefore, what passed, and was easily helped to rise; and, shaded by her packet, which, even in her first terrour, she had instinctively held to her face, she made a motion to walk into the air. One of the men, good naturedly, placed her a chair without doors; she sat upon it thankfully, and almost as quickly recovered as she had lost her force, by a reviving idea, that, even yet, thus situated, she might make her escape.

She had just risen with this view, when the voice of the pilot, who was coming round the house, from the stable-yard, forced her hastily to re-enter the passage; but not before she heard him enquire, whether a French gentleman were arrived in that chaise?

Again, now, she glided on towards the stairs; hearing, as she passed, the answer made by the French gentleman himself: '*Oui, oui, me voici. Quelles sont les nouvelles?*'[1]

The voices of both proved each to be advancing to the passage, to meet the other. Juliet was no longer sensible of bodily weakness; nor scarcely of bodily existence. She seemed to herself a mere composition of terrour. She flew up the stairs, meaning to regain her little chamber; but, mistaking her way, found herself in a gallery, leading to the best apartments. Glad, however, rather than sorry, in the hope she might here be less liable to be sought, she opened the first door; and, entering a large room, locked and bolted herself in, with such extreme precipitance, that already she had sunk upon her knees, in fervent prayer, before a shadow, which caught her eyes, made her look round; when she perceived, at a distant window, a gentleman who was writing.

In the deepest consternation, she arose, hurrying to find the key; which, in her perturbation, she had taken out, and let drop she knew not where.

While earnestly searching it, the gentleman, mildly, yet in a tone of some surprize, enquired what she wanted.

Startled at the sound of his voice, she looked up, and saw Harleigh.

Her conflicting emotions now exceeded all that she had hitherto experienced. To seem to follow, even to his room, the man whom she had adjured, as he valued her preservation, to quit and avoid her; joined sensations of shame so poignant, to those of horrour and anguish, with which she was already overwhelmed, that, almost, she wished her last hour to arrive; that, while finishing her wretchedness, she might clear her integrity and honour.

Harleigh, to whom her dress, as he had not caught a view of her face, proved a complete disguise of her person, concluded her to be some light nymph of the inn, and suffered her to search for the key, without even repeating his question: but when, upon her finding it, he observed that her shaking hand could not, for some time, fix it in the lock, he was struck with something in her general form that urged him to rise, and offer his assistance.

Still more her hand shook, but she opened the door, and, without answering, and with a head carefully averted, eagerly quitted the room; shutting herself out, with trembling precipitation.

Harleigh hesitated whether to follow; but it was only for a moment: the next, a shriek of agony reached his ears, and, hastily rushing forth, he saw the female who had just quitted him, standing in an attitude of despair; her face bowed down upon her hands; while an ill-looking man, whom he presently recollected for the pilot, grinning in triumph, and with arms wide extended, to prevent her passing, loudly called out, '*Citoyen! Citoyen! venez voir! c'est Elle! Je la tien!*'[2]

Harleigh would have remonstrated against this rude detention; but he had no sooner begun speaking, than Juliet, finding that she could not advance, retreated; and had just put her hand upon the lock of a door, higher up in the gallery; when another man, dressed with disgusting negligence, and of a hideous countenance, yet wearing an air of ferocious authority; advancing by large strides, roughly seized her arm, with one hand, while, with the other, he rudely lifted up her bonnet, to examine her face.

'*C'est bien!*' he cried, with a look of exultation, that gave to his horrible features an air of infernal joy; '*viens, citoyenne, viens; suis moi.*'[3]

Harleigh, who, when the bonnet was raised, saw, what as yet he had feared to surmise,—that it was Juliet; sprang forward, exclaiming, 'Daring ruffian! quit your hold!'

'*Ose tu nier mes droits?*' cried the man, addressing Juliet; whose arm he still griped;—'*Dis!—parles!—l'ose tu?*'[4]

Juliet was mute; but Harleigh saw that she was sinking, and bent towards her to save her fall; what, then, was his astonishment, to perceive that it was voluntary! and that she cast herself at the feet of her assailant!

Thunderstruck, he held back.

The man, with an expression of diabolical delight at this posture, cast his eyes now upon her, now upon her appalled defendant; and then, in French, gave orders to the pilot, to see four fresh horses put to the chaise: and, in a tone of somewhat abated rage, bid Juliet arise, and accompany him down stairs.

'Ah, no!—ah, spare—ah, leave me yet!—' in broken accents, and in French, cried the still prostrate Juliet.

The man, who was large made, tall, and strong, seized, then, both her arms, with a motion that indicated his intention to drag her along.

A piercing shriek forced its way from her at his touch: but she arose, and made no appeal, no remonstrance.

'*Si tu peus le conduire toute seule,*' said the man, sneeringly, '*soit! Mais vas en avant! Je ne le perdrai plus de vu.*'[5]

Juliet again hid her face, but stood still.

The man roughly gave her a push; seeming to enjoy, with a coarse laugh, the pleasure of driving her on before him.

Harleigh, who saw that her face was convulsed with horrour, fiercely planted himself in the midst of the passage, vehemently exclaiming, 'Infernal monster! by what right do you act?'

'*De quel droit me le demandez vous?*'[6] cried the man; who appeared perfectly to understand English.

'By the rights of humanity!' replied Harleigh; 'and you shall answer me by the rights of justice! One claim alone can annul my interference. Are you her father?'

'*Non!*' he answered, with a laugh of scorn; '*mais il y a d'autres droits!*'[7]

'There are none!' cried Harleigh, 'to which you can pretend; none!'

'*Comment cela? n'est-ce pas ma femme? Ne suis-je pas son mari?*'[8]

'No!' cried Harleigh, 'no!' with the fury of a man seized with sudden delirium; 'I deny it!—'tis false! and neither you nor all the fiends of hell shall make me believe it!'

Juliet again fell prostrate; but, though her form turned towards her assailant, her eyes, and supplicating hands, that begged forbearance, were lifted up, in speechless agony, to Harleigh.

Repressed by this look and action, though only to be overpowered by the blackest surmises, Harleigh again stood suspended.

Finding the people of the inn were now filling the staircase, to see what was the matter, the foreigner, in tolerable English, told them all to be gone, for he was only recovering an eloped wife. Then, addressing Juliet, 'If you dare assert,' he said, 'that you are not my wife, your perjury may cost you dear! If you have not that hardiness, hold your tongue and welcome. Who else will dare dispute my claims?'

'I will!' cried Harleigh, furiously. 'Walk this way, Sir, and give me an account of yourself! I will defend that lady from your inhuman grasp, to the last drop of my blood!'

'Ah, no! ah, no!' Juliet now faintly uttered; but the man, interrupting her, said, 'Dare you assert, I demand, that you are not my wife? Speak! Dare you?'

Again she bowed down her face upon her hands,—her face that seemed bloodless with despair; but she was mute.

'I put you to the test;' continued the man, striding to the end of the gallery, and opening the last door: 'Go into that chamber!'

She shrieked aloud with agony uncontrollable; and Harleigh, with an emotion irrepressible, cast his arms around her, exclaiming, 'Place yourself under my protection! and no violence, no power upon earth shall tear you away!'

At these words, all the force of her character came again to her aid; and she disengaged herself from him, with a reviving dignity in her air, that shewed a decided resolution to resist his services: but she was still utterly silent; and he saw that she was obliged to sustain her tottering frame against the wall, to save herself from again sinking upon the floor.

The foreigner seemed with difficulty to restrain his rage from some act of brutality; but, after a moment's pause, fixing his hands fiercely in his sides, he ferociously confronted the shaking Juliet, and said, 'I have informed your family of my rights. Lord Denmeath has promised me his assistance and your portion.'

'Lord Denmeath!' repeated the astonished Harleigh.

'He has promised me, also,' the foreigner, without heeding him, continued, 'the support of your half-brother, Lord Melbury,—'

'Lord Melbury!' again exclaimed Harleigh; with an expression that spoke a sudden delight, thrilling, in defiance of agony, through his burning veins.

'Who, he assures me, is a young man of honour, who will never abet a wife in eloping from her husband. I shall take you, therefore, at first, and at once, to Lord Denmeath, who will only pay your portion to your own signature. Go, therefore, quietly into that room, till the chaise is ready, and I promise that I won't follow you: though, if you resist, I shall assert my rights by force.'

He held the door open. She wrung her hands with agonizing horrour. He took hold of her shoulder; she shrunk from his touch; but, in shrinking, involuntarily entered the room. He would have pushed her on; but Harleigh, who now looked wild with the violence of contending emotions; with rage, astonishment, grief, and despair; furiously caught him by the arm, calling out, 'Hold, villain, hold!—Speak, Madam, speak! Utter but a syllable!—Deign only to turn towards me!—Pronounce but with your eyes that he has no legal claim, and I will instantly secure your liberty,—even from myself!—even from all mankind!—Speak!—turn!—look but a moment this way!—One word! one single word!—'

She clapped her hands upon her forehead, in an action of despair; but the word was not spoken,—not a syllable was uttered! A look, however, escaped her, expressive of a soul in torture, yet supplicating his retreat. She then stepped further into the room, and the foreigner shut and double-locked the door.

Triumphantly brandishing the key, as he eyed, sidelong, the now passive Harleigh, he went into the adjoining apartment; where, seating himself in the middle of the room, he left the door wide open, to watch all egress and regress in the passage.

Harleigh now appeared to be lost! The violence of his agitation, while he concluded her to be wrongfully claimed, was transformed into the blackest and most indignant despondence, at her unresisting, however wretched acquiescence, to commands thus brutal; emanating from an authority of which, however evidently it was deplored, she attempted not to controvert the legality. The dreadful mystery, more direful than it had been depicted, even by the most cruel of his apprehensions, was now revealed: she is married! he internally cried; married to the vilest of wretches, whom she flies and abhors, —yet she is married! indisputably married! and can never, never,—even in my wishes, now, be mine!

A sudden sensation, kindred even to hatred, took possession of his feelings. Altered she appeared to him, and delusive. She had always, indeed, discouraged his hopes, always forbidden his expectations; yet she must have seen that they subsisted, and were cherished; and could not but have been conscious, that a single word, bitter, but essentially just, might have demolished, have annihilated them in a moment.

He dragged himself back to his apartment, and resolutely shut his door; gloomily bent to nourish every unfavourable impression, that might sicken regret by resentment. But no indignation could curb his grief at her loss; nor his horrour at her situation: and the look that had compelled his retreat; the look that so expressively had concentrated and conveyed her so often reiterated sentence, of 'leave, or you destroy me!' seemed rivetted to his very brain, so as to take despotic and exclusive hold of all his faculties.

In a few minutes, the sound of a carriage almost mechanically drew him to the window. He saw there an empty chaise and four horses. It was surely to convey her away!—and with the man whom she loathed,—and from one who, so often! had awakened in her symptoms the most impressive of the most flattering sensibility!—

The transitory calm of smothered, but not crushed emotions, was now succeeded by a storm of the most violent and tragic passions. To lose her for ever, yet irresistibly to believe himself beloved!—to see her nearly lifeless with misery, yet to feel that to demand a conference, or the smallest explanation, or even a parting word, might expose her to the jealousy of a brute, who seemed capable of enjoying, rather than deprecating, any opportunity to treat her ill; to be convinced that she must be the victim of a forced marriage; yet to feel every sentiment of honour, and if of honour of happiness! rise to oppose all violation of a rite, that, once performed, must be held sacred:—thoughts, reflections, ideas thus dreadful, and sensations thus excruciating, almost deprived him of reason, and he cast himself upon the ground in wild agony.

But he was soon roused thence by the gruff voice, well recollected, of the pilot, who, from the bottom of the stairs, called out, '*Viens, citoyen! tout est pret.*'[9]

With horrour, now, he heard the heavy step of the foreigner again in the passage; he listened, and the sound reached his ear of the key fixing—the door unlocking.—Excess of torture then caused a short suspension of his faculties, and he heard no more.

Soon, however, reviving, the stillness startled him. He opened his door. No one was in the passage; but he caught a plaintive sound, from the room in which Juliet was a prisoner: and soon gathered that Juliet herself was imploring for leave to travel to Lord Denmeath's alone.

What an aggravation to the sufferings of Harleigh, to learn that she was thus allied, at the moment that he knew her to be another's! for however the violence of his admiration had conquered every obstacle, he had always thought, with reluctance and concern, of the supposed obscurity of her family and connections.

Juliet pleaded in vain. A harsh refusal was followed by the grossest menace, if she hesitated to accompany him at once.

The pilot, repeating his call, now mounted the stairs; and Harleigh felt compelled to return to his room; but, looking back in re-entering it, he saw Juliet forced into the passage; her face not merely pale, but ghastly; her eyes nearly starting from her head.

To rescue, to protect her, Harleigh now thought was all that could render life desirable; but, while adoring her almost to madness, he respected her situation and her fame, and re-passed into his chamber, unseen by the foreigner.

Yet he could not forbear placing himself so that he might catch a glance of her as she went by; he held the door, therefore, in his hand, as if, accidentally, at that moment, opening it. She did not turn her head, but assumed an air of resignation, and walked straight on; yet though she did not meet his eye, she evidently felt it; a pale pink suffusion shot across her cheeks; taking place of the death-like hue they had exhibited as she quitted her room; but which, fading away almost in the same moment, left her again a seeming spectre.

A nervous dimness took from Harleigh even the faculty of observing the foreigner. She loves me! was his thought; she surely loves me! And the idea which, not many minutes sooner, would have chaced from his mind every feeling but of felicity, now rent his heart with torture, from painting their mutual unhappiness. It was not a sigh that he stifled, nor a sigh that escaped him; but a groan, a piercing groan, which broke from his sorrows, as he heard her tottering step reach the stairs, while internally he uttered, She is gone from me for ever!

When he thought she would no longer be in sight, he followed to the first landing-place; to catch, once more, even the most distant sound of her feet: but the passage to and fro of waiters, forced him again to mount to his chamber. There, he hastened to the window, to take a view, a last view! of her loved form; but thence, shuddering, retreated, at sight of the chaise and four; destined to whirl her everlastingly away from him, with a companion so undisguisedly dreaded!—so evidently abhorred!

Yet, at the first sound, he returned to the window; whence he perceived Juliet just arrived upon the threshold; looking like a picture of death, and leaning upon a chambermaid, to whom she clung as to a bosom friend; yet not attempting to resist the foreigner; who, on her other side, dragged her by the arm, in open triumph. But, when she came to the chaise-step, she staggered, her vital powers seemed forsaking her; she heaved a hard and painful sigh, and, but for the chambermaid, who knelt down to catch her, had fallen upon the ground.

Harleigh was already half way down the stairs, almost frantic to save her; before he had sufficient recollection to remind him, that any effort on his part might cause her yet grosser insult. He was then again at his window; where he saw a second chambermaid administering burnt feathers, which had already recovered her from the fainting fit; while the mistress of the house was presenting her with hartshorn and water.

She refused no assistance; but the foreigner, who was loudly enraged at the delay, said that he would lift her into the chaise; and bid the pilot get in first, to help the operation.

She now again looked so sick and disordered, that all the women called upon the foreigner to let her re-enter the house, and take a little rest, before her journey. Her eyes, turned up to heaven with thankfulness, even at the proposal, encouraged them to grow clamorous in their demand; but the man, with a scornful sneer, replied that her journey would be her cure; and told the pilot, who was finishing a bottle of wine, to make haste.

The wretched Juliet, resuming her resolution, though with an air of despair, faintly pronounced, that she would get into the carriage herself; and, leaning upon the woman, ascended the steps, and dropt upon the seat of the chaise.

CHAPTER LXXIX

At this moment, a horseman, who had advanced full gallop, hastily dismounting, enquired aloud, whether any French gentleman had lately arrived.

All who were present, pointed to the foreigner; who, not hearing, or affecting not to hear the demand, began pushing away the women, that he might follow Juliet.

The horseman, approaching, asked the foreigner his name.

'*Qu'est ce que cela vous fait?*'[10] he answered.

'You must come with me into the inn,' the horseman replied, after stedfastly examining his face.

The foreigner, with a loud oath, refused to stir.

The horseman, holding out a paper, clapped him upon the shoulder, saying, that he was a person who had been looked for some time, in consequence of information which had been lodged against him; and that he was to be sent out of the kingdom.

This declaration made, he called upon the master of the house to lend his assistance, for keeping the arrested person in custody, till the arrival of the proper officers of justice.

The man, at first, could find no vent for his rage, except horrid oaths, and tremendous imprecations; but, when he was positively seized, with a menace of being bound hand and foot, if he offered any opposition, he swore that his wife, at least, should accompany him; and put forth his hand towards the chaise, to drag out Juliet.

But Juliet was saved from his grasp by the landlady; who humanely, upon seeing her almost expiring condition, had entered the carriage, during the dispute, with a viol of sal volatile.

The horseman, who was a peace-officer, said that he had no orders to arrest any woman. She might come, or stay, as she pleased.

The foreigner vociferously claimed her; uttering execrations against all who unlawfully withheld her; or would abet her elopement. He would then have passed round to the other door of the chaise, to seize her by force; but the peace-officer, who was habitually deaf to any appeal, and resolute against any resistance; compelled him, though storming, raging, and swearing, his face

21

distorted with fury, his under-jaw dropt, and his mouth foaming, to re-enter the inn.

Juliet received neither relief nor fresh pain from what passed. Though no longer fainting, terrour and excess of misery operated so powerfully upon her nerves, that his cries assailed her ears but as outrage upon outrage; and, though clinging to the landlady, with instinctive entreaty for support, she was so disordered by her recent fainting, and so absorbed in the belief that she was lost, that she knew not what had happened; nor suspected any impediment to her forced journey; till the landlady, now quitting her, advised her to have a room and lie down; saying that no wife could be expected to follow such a brute of a husband to jail.

Amazed, she enquired what was meant; and was answered, that her husband was in the hands of justice.

The violence of the changed, yet mixed sensations, with which she was now assailed, made every pulse throb with so palpitating a rapidity, that she felt as if life itself was seeking a vent through every swelling vein. But, when again she was pressed to enter the house, and not to accompany her husband to prison; she shuddered, her head was bowed down with shame; and, making a motion that supplicated for silence, she seemed internally torn asunder with torturing incertitude how to act.

During this instant,—it was scarcely more,—of irresolution, the landlady alighted, and the chaise was driven abruptly from the door. But Juliet had scarcely had time for new alarm, ere she found that she had only been removed to make way for another carriage; from the window of which she caught a glimpse of Sir Jaspar Herrington.

Nor had she escaped his eye; her straw-bonnet having fallen off, without being missed, while she fainted, her head was wholly without shade.

With all of speed in his power, the Baronet hobbled to the chaise. She covered her face, sinking with every species of confusion and distress. 'Have I the honour,' he cried, 'to address Miss Granville? The Honourable Miss Granville?'—

'Good Heaven!—'Juliet astonished, and raising her head, exclaimed.

'If so, I have the dulcet commission,' he continued, 'to escort her to her brother and sister, Lord Melbury, and Lady Aurora Granville.'

'Is it possible? Is it possible?' cried Juliet, in an ecstacy that seemed to renovate her whole being: 'I dare not believe it!—Oh Sir Jaspar! dear, good, kind, generous Sir Jaspar! delude me not, in pity!'

'No, fairest syren!' answered Sir Jaspar, in a rapture nearly equal to her own; 'if there be any delusion to fear, 'tis poor I must be its victim!'

'Oh take me, then, at once,—this instant,—this moment,—take me to them, my benevolent, my noble friend! If, indeed, I have a brother, a sister,—give me the heaven of their protection!—'

Sir Jaspar, enchanted, invited her to honour him by accepting a seat in his chaise. With glowing gratitude she complied; though the just returning roses faded from her cheeks, as she alighted, upon perceiving Harleigh, aloof and disconsolate, fixed like a statue, upon a small planted eminence. Yet but momentarily was the whiter hue prevalent, and her skin, the next instant, burned with blushes of the deepest dye.

This transition was not lost upon Harleigh: his eye caught, and his heart received it, with equal avidity and anguish. Ah why, thought he, so sensitive! why, at this period of despair, must I awaken to a consciousness of the full extent of my calamity! Yet, all his resentment subsided; to believe that she participated in his sentiments, had a charm so softening, so all-subduing, that, even in this crisis of torture and hopelessness, it dissolved his whole soul into tenderness.

Juliet, faintly articulating, 'Oh, let us be gone!' moved, with cast down eyes, to the carriage of the Baronet; forced, from remaining weakness, to accept the assistance of his groom; Sir Jaspar not having strength, nor Harleigh courage, to offer aid.

Sir Jaspar demanded her permission to stop at Salisbury, for his valet and baggage.

'Any where! any where!' answered the shaking Juliet, 'so I go but to Lady Aurora!'

Astonished, and thrilled to the soul by these words, Harleigh, who, unconsciously, had advanced, involuntarily repeated, 'Lady Aurora?—Lady Aurora Granville?'—

Unable to answer, or to look at him, the trembling Juliet, eagerly laying both her hands upon the arm of the Baronet, as, cautiously, he was mounting into the carriage, supplicated that they might be gone.

A petition thus seconded, from so adored a suppliant, was irresistible; he kissed each fair hand that thus honoured him; and had just accepted the offer of Harleigh, to aid his arrangements; when the furious prisoner, struggling with the peace-officers, and loudly swearing, re-appeared at the inn-door, clamorously demanding his wife.

The tortured Juliet, with an impulse of agony, cast, now, the hands that were just withdrawn from the Baronet, upon the shoulder of Harleigh, who was himself fastening the chaise-door, tremulously, and in a tone scarcely audible, pronouncing, 'Oh! hurry us away, Mr Harleigh!—in mercy!—in compassion!'

Harleigh, bowing upon the hands which he ventured not to touch, but of which he felt the impression with a pang indescribable, called to the postilion to drive off full gallop.

With a low and sad inclination of the head, Juliet, in a faultering voice, thanked him; involuntarily adding, 'My prayers, Mr Harleigh,—my every wish for happiness,—will for ever be yours!'

The chaise drove off; but his groan, rather than sigh, reached her agonized ear; and, in an emotion too violent for concealment, yet to which she durst allow no vent, she held her almost bursting forehead with her hand; breathing only by smothered sighs, and scarcely sensible to the happiness of an uncertain escape, while bowed down by the sight of the misery that she had inflicted, where all that she owed was benevolence, sympathy, and generosity.

Not even the delight of thus victoriously carrying off a disputed prize, could immediately reconcile Sir Jaspar to the fear of even the smallest disorder in the economy of his medicines, anodynes, sweetmeats, and various whims; which, from long habits of self-indulgence, he now conceived to be necessaries, not luxuries.

But when, after having examined, in detail, that his travelling apparatus was in order, he turned smilingly to the fair mede of his exertions; and saw the deep absorption of all her faculties in her own evident affliction, he was struck with surprise and disappointment; and, after a short and mortified pause, 'Can it be, fair ænigma!' he cried, 'that it is with compunction you abandon this Gallic Goliah?'

Surprised, through this question, from the keen anguish of speechless suffering; retrospection and anticipation alike gave way to gratitude, and she poured forth her thanks, her praises, and her wondering delight, at this unexpected, and marvellous rescue, with so much vivacity of transport, and so much softness of sensibility for his kindness, that the enchanted Sir Jaspar, losing all forbearance, in the interest with which he languished to learn, more positively, her history and her situation, renewed his entreaties for communication, with an urgency that she now, for many reasons, no longer thought right to resist: anxious herself, since concealment was at an end, to clear away the dark appearances by which she was surrounded; and to remove a mystery that, for so long a period, had made her owe all good opinion to trust and generosity.

She pondered, nevertheless, and sighed, ere she could comply. It was strange to her, she said, and sad, to lift up the veil of secresy to a new, however interesting and respectable acquaintance; while to her brother, her sister, and her earliest friend, she still appeared to be inveloped in impenetrable concealment. Yet, if to communicate the circumstances which had brought her into this deplorable situation, could shew her sense of the benevolence of Sir Jaspar, she would set apart her repugnance, and gather courage to retrace the cruel scenes of which he had witnessed the direful result. Her inestimable friend had already related the singular history of all that had preceded their separation; but, uninformed herself of the dreadful events by which it had been followed, she could go no further: otherwise, from a noble openness of heart, which made all disguise painful, if not disgusting to her, Sir Jaspar would already have been satisfied.

The Baronet, ashamed, would now have withdrawn his petition; but Juliet no longer wished to retract from her engagement.

CHAPTER LXXX

The first months after the departure of Gabriella, were passed, Juliet narrated, quietly, though far from gaily, in complete retirement. To lighten, through her cares and services, the terrible change of condition experienced by her benefactress, the Marchioness, and by her guardian, the Bishop, was her unremitting, and not successless endeavour: but even this sad tranquillity was soon broken in upon, by an accidental interview with a returned emigrant, who brought news of the dangerous state of health into which the young son of Gabriella had fallen. Too well knowing that this cherished little creature was the sole consolation and support of its exiled mother, the Marchioness earnestly desired that her daughter should possess again her early companion; who best could aid to nurse the child; or, should its illness prove fatal, to render its loss supportable. It was, therefore, settled, that, guarded and accompanied by a faithful ancient servant, upon whose prudence and attachment the Marchioness had the firmest reliance, Juliet should follow her friend: and the benevolent Bishop promised to join them both, as soon as his affairs would permit him to make the voyage.

To obtain a passport being then impossible, Ambroise, this worthy domestic, was employed to discover means for secretly crossing the channel: and, as adroit as he was trusty, he found out a pilot, who, though ostensibly but a fisherman, was a noted smuggler; and who passed frequently to the opposite shore; now with goods, now with letters, now with passengers. By this man the Marchioness wrote to prepare Gabriella for the reception of her friend, who was to join her at Brighthelmstone; whither, in her last letter, written, as Juliet now knew, in the anguish of discovering symptoms of danger in the illness of her darling boy, Gabriella had mentioned her intended excursion for sea-bathing. The diligent Ambroise soon obtained information that the pilot was preparing to sail with a select party. The Marchioness would rather have postponed the voyage, till an answer could have been received from her daughter; yet this was not an opportunity to be neglected.

The light baggage, therefore, was packed, and they were waiting the word of command from the pilot, when a commissary, from the Convention, arrived, to purify, he said, and new-organize the town, near which, in a villa that had been a part of her marriage-portion, the Marchioness and her brother then resided. To this villa the commissary made his first visit. The Bishop, by this agent of the inhuman Robespierre, was immediately seized; and, while his unhappy sister, and nearly adoring ward, were vainly kneeling at the feet of his condemner,—not accuser! to supplicate mercy for innocence,—not for guilt! the persons who were rifling the Bishop, shouted out, with savage joy, that they had found a proof of his being a traitor, in a note in his pocket-book, which was clearly a bribe from the enemy to betray the country. The commissary, who, having often been employed as a spy, had a competent knowledge of modern languages, which he spoke intelligibly, though with vulgar phraseology and accent; took the paper, and read it without difficulty. It was the promissory note of the old Earl Melbury.

He eagerly demanded the Citoyenne Julie; swearing that, if six thousand pounds were to be got by marrying, he would marry without delay. He ordered her, therefore, to accompany him forthwith to the mayoralty. At her indignant refusal, he scoffingly laughed; but, upon her positive resistance, ordered her into custody. This, also, moved her not; she only begged to be confined in the same prison with the Bishop. Coarsely mocking her attachment for the priest, and holding her by the chin, he swore that he would marry her, and her six thousand pounds.

A million of deaths, could she die them, she resolutely replied, she would suffer in preference.

Her priest, then, he said, should away to the guillotine; though she had only to marry, and sign the promissory-note for the dower, to set the parson at liberty. Filled with horrour, she wrung her hands, and stood suspended; while the Marchioness, with anguish indescribable, and a look that made a supplication that no voice could pronounce, fell upon her neck, gasping for breath, and almost fainting.

'Ah, Madam!' Juliet cried, 'what is your will? I am yours,—entirely yours! command me!'—

The Marchioness could not speak; but her sighs, her groans, rather, were more eloquent than any words.

'Bind the priest!' the commissary cried. 'His trial is over; bind the traitor, and take him to the cell for execution.'

The Marchioness sunk to the floor.

'No!' cried Juliet, 'bind him not! Touch not his reverend and revered person! —Give me the paper! I will sign what you please! I will go whither you will!'

'Come, then,' cried the commissary, 'to the mayoralty.'

Juliet covered her face, but moved towards the door.

The Bishop, hitherto passive and meekly resigned, now, with a sudden effort of strength, repulsing his gaolers, while fire darted from his eyes, and a spirit of command animated all his features, exclaimed, 'No, generous Juliet! my own excellent child, no! Are a few years more or less,—perhaps but a few minutes,—worth purchasing by the sacrifice of truth, and the violation of every feeling? I will not be saved upon such terms!'

'No preaching,' cried the commissary; 'off with him at once.'

The men now bound his hands and arms; while, returning to his natural state of calmness, he lifted up his eyes towards heaven, and, in a loud and sonorous voice, ejaculated, in Latin, a fervent prayer; with an air so absorbed in mental and pious abstraction, that he seemed unconscious what became of his person.

Juliet, who had shrunk back at his speech, again advanced, and, with agony unspeakable, held out her hand, in token of consent. The commissary received it triumphantly, at the moment that the Bishop, upon reaching the door, turned round to take a last view of his unhappy sister; who, torn with conflicting emotions, seemed a statue of horror. But no sooner did he perceive the hand of his ward unresistingly grasped by the commissary, than again the expression of his face shewed his soul brought back from its heavenly absorption; and, stopping short, with an air which, helpless and shackled as he was, overawed his fierce conductors, 'Hold yet a moment,' he cried. 'Oh Juliet! Think,—know what you are about! 'Tis not to this world alone you are responsible for vows offered up at the altar of God! My child! my more than daughter! sacrifice not your purity to your affections! Drag me not back from a virtuous death to a miserable existence, by the foul crime of wilful perjury!'

Juliet affrighted, again snatched away her hand, with a look at the commissary which pronounced an abhorrent refusal.

The commissary, stamping with fury, ordered the Bishop instantly to the cell of death. Where guilt, he said, had been proved, there was no need of any tribunal; and the execution should take place with the speed called for by his dangerous crimes.

Juliet, cold, trembling, and again irresolute, was involuntarily turning to the commissary; but the Bishop, charging her to be firm, pronounced a pious blessing upon her head; faintly spoke a last adieu to his miserable sister, and, with commanding solemnity, accompanied his gaolers away.

The horrour of that moment Juliet attempted not to describe; nor could she recur to it, without sighs and emotions that, for a while, stopt her narration.

Sir Jaspar would have spared her the resumption of the history; but she would not, having thus raised, trifle with his curiosity.

The commissary, she continued, then took possession of all the money, plate, and jewels he could find, and pursued what he called his rounds of purification.

How the Marchioness or herself out-lived that torturing day, Juliet declared she could with difficulty, now, conceive. She was again willing to become a victim to the safety of her guardian; but even the Marchioness ceased to desire his preservation upon terms from which he himself recoiled as culpable. Early the next morning they were both conducted to a large house upon the market-place, where, in the most direful suspense, they were kept waiting for more than two hours; in which interval, such was the oppression of terrour, neither of them opened their lips.

The commissary, at length, broke into the room, and, seating himself in an arm-chair, while, humbly and tremblingly, they stood at the door, demanded of Juliet whether she were become more reasonable. Her head drooped, but she would not answer. 'Follow me,' he cried, 'to this balcony.' He opened a door leading to a large apartment that looked upon the market-place. She suspected some sinister design, and would not obey. 'Come you, then!' he cried, to the Marchioness; and, taking her by the shoulder, rudely and grossly, he pushed her before him, till she entered upon the balcony. A dreadful scream, which then broke from her, brought Juliet to her side.

Here, again, overpowered by the violence of bitter recollections, which operated, for the moment, with nearly the force of immediate suffering, Juliet was obliged to take breath before she could proceed.

'Oh Sir Jaspar!' she then cried, 'upon approaching the wretched Marchioness, what a distracting scene met my eyes! A scaffolding,—a guillotine,—an executioner,—were immediately opposite me! and in the hand of that hardened executioner, was held up to the view of the senseless multitude, the ghastly, bleeding head of a victim that moment offered up at the shrine of unmeaning though ferocious cruelty! Four other destined victims, kneeling and devoutly at prayers, their hands tied behind them, and their heads bald, were prepared for sacrifice; and amidst them, eminently conspicuous, from his dignified mien, and pious calmness, I distinguished my revered guardian! the Marchioness had distinguished her beloved brother!—Oh moment of horrour exceeding all description! I cast myself, nearly frantic, at the feet of the commissary; I embraced his knees, as if with the fervour of affection; wildly and passionately I conjured him to accept my hand and fortune, and save the Bishop!—He laughed aloud with triumphant derision; but gave an immediate order to postpone the execution of the priest. I blest him,—yes, with all his crimes upon his head!—and even again I should bless him, to save a life so precious!

'The Marchioness, recovering her strength with her hopes, seized the arm of the messenger of this heavenly news, hurrying him along with a force nearly supernatural, and calling out aloud herself, from the instant that she entered the market place, "*Un sursit! Un sursit!*"[111]

"'Now, then," cried the commissary, "come with me to the mayoralty;" and was taking my no longer withheld, but shaking hand, when some soldiers abruptly informed him than an insurrection had broken out at ——, which demanded his immediate presence.

'I caught this moment of his engaged attention to find my way down stairs, and into the market-place: but not with a view to escape; every feeling of my soul was concentrated in the safety of the Bishop. I rushed forward, I forced my way through the throng, which, though at first it opposed my steps, no sooner looked at me than, intimidated by my desperation, or affected by my agony, it facilitated my passage. Rapidly I overtook the Marchioness, whose age, whose dignified energy, and loud cries of Reprieve! made way for her through every impediment, whether of crowd or of guards, to the scaffolding. How we accomplished it, nevertheless, I now wonder! But a sense of right, when asserted with courage, is lodged in the lowest, the vilest of mankind;—a sense of right, an awe of justice, and a propensity to sympathize with acute distress! The reprieve which our cries had anticipated, and which the man whom we accompanied confirmed, was received by the multitude, from an ardent and universal respect to the well known excellencies of the Bishop, with shouts of applause that exalted our joy at his deliverance into a felicity which we thought celestial! At his venerable feet we prostrated ourselves, as if he had been a martyr to religion, and already was sainted. He was greatly affected; though perhaps only by our emotion; for he looked too uncertain how this event had been brought to bear, to partake of our happiness; and at me he cast an eye so full of compassion, yet so interrogative, that mine sunk under it; and, far from exulting that I had thus devoted myself to his preservation, I was already trembling at the acknowledgement I had to make, when I was suddenly seized by a soldier, who forced me, from all the tenderest interests of my heart, back to the stormy commissary. Oh! what a change of scene! He roughly took me by the arm, which felt as if it were withered, and no longer a part of my frame at his touch; and, with accusations of the grossest nature, and vows the most tremendous of vengeance, compelled me to attend him to the mayoralty; deaf to my prayers, my entreaties, my kneeling supplications that he would first suffer me to see the Bishop at liberty.

'At the mayoralty he was accosted by a messenger sent from the Convention. Ah! it seemed to me, at that moment, that a whole age of suffering could not counterbalance the delight I experienced, when, to read an order thus presented to him, he was constrained to relinquish his hard grasp! Still greater was my relief, when I learnt, by what passed, that he had received commands to proceed directly to ———, where the insurrection was become dangerous.

'Such a multiplicity of business now crowded upon him, that I conceived a hope I might be forgotten; or, at least, set apart as a future prey: but alas! the promissory-note was still in his hand, and,—if heart he has any,—if heart be not left out in his composition, there, past all doubt, the six thousand pounds were already lodged. All my hopes, therefore, faded away, when he had given some new directions; for, seizing me again, by the wrist, he dragged me to the place,—I had nearly said of execution!—There, by his previous orders, all were in waiting,—all was ready!—Oh, Sir Jaspar! how is it that life still holds, in those periods when all our earthly hopes, and even our faculties of happiness, seem for ever entombed.'

The bitterest sighs again interrupted her narration; but neither the humanity nor the politeness of Sir Jaspar could combat any longer his curiosity, and he conjured her to proceed.

'The civil ceremony, dreadful, dreadful! however little awful compared with that of the church, was instantly begun; in the midst of the buz of business, the clamour of many tongues, the sneers of contempt, and the laughter of derision; with an irreverence that might have suited a theatre, and with a mockery of which the grossest buffoons would have been ashamed. Scared and disordered, I understood not,—I heard not a word; and my parched lips, and burning mouth, could not attempt any articulation.

'In a minute or two, this pretended formality was interrupted, by information that a new messenger from the Convention demanded immediate admittance. The commissary swore furiously that he should wait till the six thousand pounds were secured; and vociferously ordered that the ceremony should be hurried on. He was obeyed! and though my quivering lips were never opened to pronounce an assenting syllable, the ceremony, the direful ceremony, was finished, and I was called,—Oh heaven and earth!—his wife! his married wife!—The Marchioness, at the same terrible moment, broke into the apartment. The conflict between horrour and tenderness was too violent, and, as she encircled me, with tortured pity, in her arms, I sunk senseless at her feet.

'Upon recovering, the first words that I heard were, "Look up, my child, look up! we are alone!" and I beheld the unhappy Marchioness, whose face seemed a living picture of commiserating woe. The commissary had been forced away by a new express; but he had left a charge that I should be ready to give my signature upon his return. The Marchioness then, with expressions melting, at once, and exalting, condescended to pour forth the most soothing acknowledgments; yet conjured me not to leave my own purpose unanswered, by signing the promissory-note, till the Bishop should be restored to liberty, with a passport, by which he might instantly quit this spot of persecution. To find something was yet to be done, and to be done for the Bishop, once more revived me; and when the commissary re-entered the apartment, neither order nor menace could intimidate me to take the pen, till my conditions were fulfilled. My life, indeed, at that horrible period, had lost all value but what was attached to the Bishop, the Marchioness, and my beloved Gabriella; for myself, it seemed, thenceforth, reserved not for wretchedness, but despair!

'The passport was soon prepared; but when the Bishop was brought in to receive it in my presence, he rejected it, even with severity, till he heard,—from myself heard!—that the marriage-ceremony, as it was called! was already over. Into what a consternation was he then flung! Pale grew his reverend visage, and his eyes glistened with tears. He would not, however, render abortive the sacrifice which he could no longer impede, and I signed the promissory-note; while the Marchioness wept floods of tears upon my neck; and the Bishop, with a look of anguish that rent my heart, waved, with speechless sorrow, his venerable hand, in token of a blessing, over my head; and, deeply sighing, silently departed.

'The commissary, forced immediately away, to transact some business with his successor at this place, committed me to the charge of the mayor. I was shewn to a sumptuous apartment; which I entered with a shuddering dread that the gloomiest prison could scarcely have excited. The Marchioness followed her brother; and I remained alone, trembling, shaking, almost fainting at every sound, in a state of terrour and misery indescribable. The commissary, however, returned not; and the mayor, to whom my title of horrour was a title of respect, paid me attentions of every sort.

'In the afternoon, the Marchioness brought me the reviving tidings that the Bishop was departed. He had promised to endeavour to join Gabriella. The rest of this direful day passed, and no commissary appeared: but the anguish of unremitting expectation kept aloof all joy at his absence, for, in idea, he appeared every moment! Nevertheless, after sitting up together the whole fearful night, we saw the sun rise the next morning without any new horrour. I then received a visit from the mayor, with information that the insurrection at —— had obliged the commissary to repair thither, and that he had just sent orders that I should join him in the evening. Resistance was out of the question. The tender Marchioness demanded leave to accompany me; but the mayor interposed, and forced her home, to prepare and deliver my wardrobe for the journey. It was so long ere she returned, that the patience of the mayor was almost exhausted; but when, at last, she arrived, what a change was there in her air! Her noble aspect had recovered more than its usual serenity; it was radiant with benevolence and pleasure; and, when we were left an instant together, "My Juliet!" she cried, while beaming smiles illumined her fine face, "my Juliet! my other child! blessed be Heaven, I can now rescue our rescuer! I have found means to snatch her from this horrific thraldom, in the very journey destined for its accomplishment!"

'She then briefly prepared me for meeting and seconding the scheme of deliverance that she had devised with the excellent Ambroise; and we separated,—with what tears, what regret,—yet what perturbation of rising hope!

'All that the Marchioness had arranged was executed. Ambroise, disguised as an old waggoner, preceded me to the small town of ——, where the postilion, he knew, must stop to water the horses. Here I obtained leave to alight for some refreshment, of which an old municipal officer, who had me in charge, was not sorry, in idea, to partake; as he could not entertain the most distant notion that I had formed any plan of escape. As soon, however, as I was able to disengage myself from his sight, a chambermaid, who had previously been gained by Ambroise, wrapt me in a man's great coat, put on me a black wig, and a round hat, and, pointing to a back door, went out another way; speaking aloud, as if called; to give herself the power of asserting, afterwards, that the evasion had been effected in her absence. The pretended waggoner then took me under his arm, and flew with me across a narrow passage, where we met, by appointment, an ancient domestic of the Bishop's; who conveyed me to a small house, and secreted me in a dark closet, of which the entrance was not discernible. He then went forth upon his own affairs, into such streets and places as were most public; and my good waggoner found means to abscond.

'Here, while rigidly retaining the same posture, and scarcely daring to breathe any more than to move, I heard the house entered by sundry police-officers, who were pursuing me with execrations. They came into the very room in which I was concealed; and beat round the wainscot in their search; touching even the board which covered the small aperture, not door, by which I was hidden from their view! I was not, however, discovered; nor was the search, there, renewed; from the adroitness of the domestic by whom I had been saved, in having shewn himself in the public streets before I had yet been missed.

'In this close recess, nearly without air, wholly without motion, and incapable of taking any rest; but most kindly treated by the wife of the good domestic, I passed a week. All search in that neighbourhood being then over, I changed my clothing for some tattered old garments; stained my face, throat, and arms; and, in the dead of the night, quitted my place of confinement, and was conducted by my protector to a spot about half a mile from the town. There I found Ambroise awaiting me, with a little cart; in which he drove me to a small mean house, in the vicinity of the sea-coast. He introduced me to the landlord and landlady as his relation, and then left me to take some repose; while he went forth to discover whether the pilot were yet sailed.

'He had delivered to me my work-bag, in which was my purse, generously stored by the Marchioness, with all the ready money that she could spare, for my journey. For herself, she held it essential to remain stationary, lest a general emigration should alienate the family-fortune from every branch of her house. Excellent lady! At the moment she thus studied the prosperity of her descendants, she lived upon roots, while deprived of all she most valued in life, the society of her only child!

'To repose the good Ambroise left me; but far from my pillow was repose! the dreadful idea of flying one who might lay claim to the honoured title of husband for pursuing me; the consciousness of being held by an engagement which I would not fulfil, yet could not deny; the uncertainty whether my revered Bishop had effected his escape; and the necessity of abandoning my generous benefactress when surrounded by danger; joined to the affliction of returning to my native country,—the country of my birth, my heart, and my pride!—without name, without fortune, without friends! no parents to receive me, no protector to counsel me; unacknowledged by my family,—unknown even to the children of my father!—Oh! bitter, bitter were my feelings!—Yet when I considered that no action of my life had offended society, or forfeited my rights to benevolence, I felt my courage revive, for I trusted in Providence. Sleep then visited my eye-lids, though hard was the bed upon which I sought it; hard and cold! the month was December. Happy but short respite of forgetfulness! Four days and nights followed, of the most terrible anxiety, ere Ambroise returned. He then brought me the dismaying intelligence, that circumstances had intervened, in his own affairs, that made it impossible for him, at that moment, to quit his country. Yet less than ever could my voyage be delayed, the commissary having, in his fury, advertised a description of my person, and set a price upon my head; publicly vowing that I should be made over to the guillotine, when found, for an example. Oh reign so justly called of terrour! How lawless is its cruelty! How blest by all mankind will be its termination.

'It now became necessary to my safety, that Ambroise, who was known to be a domestic of the Marchioness, should not appear to belong to me; and that, to avoid any suspicion that I was the person advertised by the commissary, I should present myself to the pilot as an accidental passenger.

'Ambroise had found means, during his absence, to communicate with the Marchioness; from whom he brought me a letter of the sweetest kindness; and intelligence and injunctions of the utmost importance.

'The commissary, she informed me, immediately upon my disappearance, had presented the promissory-note to the bankers; but they had declared it not to be valid, till it were either signed by the heir of the late Earl Melbury, or re-signed, with a fresh date, by Lord Denmeath. The commissary, therefore, had sent over an agent to Lord Denmeath, to claim, as my husband, the six thousand pounds, before my evasion should be known. The Marchioness conjured me, nevertheless, to forbear applying to my family; or avowing my name, or my return to my native land, till I should be assured of the safety of the Bishop; whom the commissary had now ordered to be pursued, and upon whom the most horrible vengeance might be wreaked, should my escape to this happy land transpire, before his own should be effected: though, while I was still supposed to be within reach of our cruel persecutor, the Bishop, even if he were seized, might merely be detained as an hostage for my future concession; till happier days, or partial accident, might work his deliverance.

'Inviolably I have adhered to these injunctions. In a note which I left for the Marchioness, with Ambroise, I solemnly assured her, that no hardships of adversity, nor even any temptation to happiness, should make me waver in my given faith; or tear from me the secret of my name and story, till I again saw, or received tidings of the Bishop. And Oh how light, how even blissful,—in remembrance, at least,—will prove every sacrifice, should the result be the preservation of the most pious and exemplary of men! But, alas! I have been discovered, while still in the dark as to his destiny, by means which no self-denial could preclude, no fortitude avert!

'The indefatigable Ambroise had learned that the pilot was to sail the next evening for Dover. I now added patches and bandages to my stained skin, and garb of poverty; and stole, with Ambroise, to the sea-side; where we wandered till past midnight; when Ambroise descried a little vessel, and the pilot; and, soon afterwards, sundry passengers, who, in dead silence, followed each other into the boat. I then approached, and called out to beg admission. I desired Ambroise to be gone; but he was too anxious to leave me. Faithful, excellent creature! how he suffered while I pleaded in vain! how he rejoiced when one of the passengers, open to heavenly pity, humanely returned to the shore to assist me into the boat! Ambroise took my last adieu to the Marchioness; and I set sail for my loved, long lost, and fearfully recovered native land.

'The effect upon my spirits of this rescue from an existence of unmingled horrour, was so exhilarating, so exquisite, that no sooner was my escape assured, than, from an impulse irresistible, I cast my ring, which I had not yet dared throw away, into the sea; and felt as if my freedom were from that moment restored! And, though innumerable circumstances were unpleasant in the way, I was insensible to all but my release; and believed that only to touch the British shore would be liberty and felicity!

'Little did I then conceive, impossible was it I should foresee, the difficulties, dangers, disgraces, and distresses towards which I was plunging! Too, too soon was I drawn from my illusion of perfect happiness! and my first misfortune was the precursor of every evil by which I have since been pursued;—I lost my purse; and, with it, away flew my fancied independence, my ability to live as I pleased, and to devote all my thoughts and my cares to consoling my beloved friend!

'Vainly in London, and vainly at Brighthelmstone I sought that friend. I would have returned to the capital, to attempt tracing her by minuter enquiry; but I was deterred by poverty, and the fear of personal discovery. I could only, therefore, continue on the spot named by the Marchioness for our general rendezvous, where the opening of every day gave me the chance of some direction how to proceed. But alas! from that respected Marchioness two letters only have ever reached me! The first assured me that she was safe and well, and that the Bishop, though forced to take a distant route, had escaped his pursuers: but that the commissary was in hourly augmenting rage, from Lord Denmeath's refusing to honour the promissory-note, till the marriage should be authenticated by the bride, with the signature and acquittal of the Bishop. The second letter,—second and last from this honoured lady!—said that all was well; but bid me wait with patience, perhaps to a long period, for further intelligence, and console and seek to dwell with her Gabriella: or, should any unforeseen circumstances inevitably separate us, endeavour to fix myself in some respectable and happy family, whose social felicity might bring, during this dread interval of suspense, reflected happiness to my own heart: but still to remain wholly unknown, till I should be joined by the Bishop.

'Cast thus upon myself, and for a time indefinite, how hardly, and how variously have I existed! But for the dreadful fear of worse, darkly and continually hovering over my head, I could scarcely have summoned courage for my unremitting trials. But whatever I endured was constantly light in comparison with what I had escaped! Yet how was I tried,—Oh Sir Jaspar! how cruelly! in resisting to present myself to my family! in forbearing to pronounce the kind appellation of brother! the soft, tender title of sister! Oh! in their sight, when witnessing their goodness, when blest by their kindness, and urged by the most generous sweetness to confidence, how violent, how indescribable have been my struggles, to withhold from throwing myself into their arms, with the fair, natural openness of sisterly affection! But Lord Denmeath, who disputed, or denied, my relation to their family, was their uncle and guardian. To him to make myself known, would have been to blight every hope of concealment from the commissary, whose claims were precisely in unison with the plan of his lordship, for making me an alien to my country. What, against their joint interests and authority, would be the power of a sister or a brother under age? Often, indeed, I was tempted to trust them in secret; and oh how consolatory to my afflicted heart would have been such a trust! but they had yet no establishment, and they were wards of my declared enemy. How unavailing, therefore, to excite their generous zeal, while necessarily forced to exact that our ties of kindred should remain unacknowledged? Upon their honour I could rely; but by their feelings, their kind, genuine, ardent feelings, I must almost unavoidably have been betrayed.

'To my Gabriella, also, I have forborne to unbosom my sorrows, and reveal my alarms, that I might spare her already so deeply wounded soul, the restless solicitude of fresh and cruel uncertainties. She concludes, that though her letters have miscarried, or been lost, her honoured mother and uncle still reside safely together, in the villa of the Marchioness, in which she had bidden them adieu. And that noble mother charged me to hide, if it should be possible, from her unhappy child, the terrible history in which I had borne so considerable a part, till she could give assurances to us both of her own and the Bishop's safety. Alas! nine months have now worn away since our separation, yet no news arrives!—no Bishop appears!

'And now, Sir Jaspar, you have fully before you the cause and history of my long concealment, my strange wanderings, and the apparently impenetrable mystery in which I have been involved: why I could not claim my family; why I could not avow my situation; why I dared not even bear my name; all, all is before you! Oh! could I equally display to you the events in store! tell you whether my revered Bishop is safe!—or whether his safety, his precious life, can only be secured by my perpetual captivity! One thing alone, in the midst of my complicate suspenses, one thing alone is certain; no consideration that this world can offer, will deter me from going back, voluntarily, to every evil from which I have hitherto been flying, should the Bishop again be seized, and should his release hang upon my final self-devotion!'

CHAPTER LXXXI

Sir Jaspar had listened to this narrative with trembling interest, and a species of emotion that was indefinable; his head bent forward, and his mouth nearly as wide open, from the fear of losing a word, as his eyes, from eagerness not to lose a look: but, when it was finished, he exclaimed, in a sort of transport, 'Is this all? Joy, then, to great Cæsar! Why 'tis nothing! My little fairies are all skipping in ecstacy; while the wickeder imps are making faces and wry mouths, not to see mischief enough in the wind to afford them a supper! This a marriage? Why you are free as air!

> 'The little birds that fly,
> With careless ease, from tree to tree,'

are not more at liberty. Ah! fair enslaver! were I as unshackled!'—

The smiles that, momentarily, broke their way through the tears and sadness of Juliet shewed how much this declaration was in unison with her wishes; but, exhausted by relating a history so deeply affecting to her, she could enter into no discussion; and remained ceaselessly weeping, till the Baronet, with an expression of surprize, asked whether the meeting that would now ensue with her own family, could offer her no consolation?

Rousing, then, from her sorrows, to a grateful though forced exertion, 'Oh yes!' she cried, 'yes! Your generous goodness has given me new existence! But horrour and distress have pursued me with such accumulating severity, that the shock is still nearly overpowering. Yet,—let me not diminish the satisfaction of your beneficence. I am going now to be happy!—How big a word!—how new to my feelings!—A sister!—a brother!—Have I, indeed, such relations?' smiling even brightly through her tears. 'And will Lady Aurora,—the sweetest of human beings!—condescend to acknowledge me? Will the amiable Lord Melbury deign to support, to protect me? Oh Sir Jaspar, how have you brought all this to bear? Where are these dearest persons? And when, and by what means, am I to be blest with their sight, and honoured with their sanction to my claim of consanguinity?'

Sir Jaspar begged her to compose her spirits, promising to satisfy her when she should become more calm. But, her thoughts having once turned into this channel, all her tenderest affections gushed forth to oppose their being diverted into any other; and the sound, the soul-penetrating sound of sister!— of brother! once allowed utterance, vibrated through her frame with a thousand soft emotions, now first welcomed without check to her heart.

Urgently, therefore, she desired an explanation of the manner in which this commission had been given; of the tone of voice in which she had been named; and of the time and place destined for the precious meeting.

Sir Jaspar, though enchanted to see her revived, and enraptured to give ear to her thanks, and to suck in her praises, was palpably embarrassed how to answer her enquiries; which he suffered her to continue so long without interruption or reply, that, her eagerness giving way to anxiety, she solemnly required to know, whether it were by accident, or through his own information, that Lord Melbury and Lady Aurora had been made acquainted with her rights, or, more properly, with her hopes and her fears in regard to their kindness and support.

Still no answer was returned, but smiling looks, and encouraging assurances.

The most alarming doubts now disturbed the just opening views of Juliet 'Ah! Sir Jaspar!' she cried, 'why this procrastination? Practise no deception, I conjure you!—Alas, you make me fear that you have acted commission?'—

He protested, upon his honour, that that was not the case; yet asked why she had settled that his commission came from Lady Aurora, or Lord Melbury?

'Good Heaven!'—exclaimed Juliet, astonished and affrighted.

He had only, he said, affirmed, that his commission was to take her to those noble personages; not that it had been from themselves that it had emanated.

Again every feature of Juliet seemed changed by disappointment; and the accent of reproach was mingled with that of grief, as she pronounced, 'Oh Sir Jaspar! can you, then, have played with my happiness? have trifled with my hopes?'—

'Not to be master of the whole planetary system,' he cried, 'with Venus, in her choicest wiles, at its head! I have honourably had my commission; but it has been for, not from your honourable relations. Those little invisible, but active beings, who have taken my conscience in charge, have spurred and goaded me on to this deed, ever since I saw your distress at the fair Gallic needle-monger's. Night and day have they pinched me and jirked me, to seek you, to find you, and to rescue you from that brawny caitiff.'—

'Alas! to what purpose? If I have no asylum, what is my security?—'

'If I have erred, my beauteous fugitive,' said Sir Jaspar, archly, 'I must order the horses to turn about! We shall still, probably, be in time to accompany the happy captive to his cell.'

Juliet involuntarily screamed, but besought, at least, to know how she had been traced; and what had induced the other pursuit; or caused the seizure, which she had so unexpectedly witnessed, of her persecutor?

He answered, that, restless to fathom a mystery, the profundity of which left, to his active imagination, as much space for distant hope as for present despair, he had invited Riley to dinner, upon quitting Frith Street; and, through his means, had discovered the pilot; whose friendship and services were secured, without scruple, by a few guineas. By this man, Sir Jaspar was shewn the advertisement, which he now produced; and which Juliet, though nearly overcome with shame, begged to read.

'ELOPED from her HUSBAND,

'A young woman, tall, fair, blue-eyed; her face oval; her nose Grecian; her mouth small; her cheeks high coloured; her chin dimpled; and her hair of a glossy light brown.

'She goes commonly by the name of Miss Ellis.

'Whoever will send an account where she may be met with, or where she has been seen, to —— Attorney in —— Street London, shall receive a very handsome reward.'

The pilot further acknowledged to Sir Jaspar, that his employer had, formerly, been at the head of a gang of smugglers and swindlers; though, latterly, he had been engaged in business of a much more serious nature.

This intelligence, with an internal conviction that the marriage must have been forced, decided Sir Jaspar to denounce the criminal to justice; and then to take every possible measure, to have him either imprisoned for trial, or sent out of the country, by the alien-bill, before he should overtake the fair fugitive. His offences were, it seems, notorious, and the warrant for his seizure was readily granted; with an order for his being embarked by the first opportunity: nevertheless, the difficulty to discover him had almost demolished the scheme: though the Baronet had aided the search in person, to enjoy the bliss of being the first to announce freedom to the lovely Runaway; and to offer her immediate protection.

But the pilot, who, after being well paid for his information, had himself absconded, delayed all proceedings till he was found out, by Riley, upon the Salisbury-road. He evaded giving any further intelligence, till the glitter of a few guineas restored his spirit of communication, when he was brought to confess, that his master was in that neighbourhood; where they had received assurances that the fugitive herself was lodged. Sir Jaspar instantly, then, took the measures of which the result, seconded by sundry happy accidents, had been so seasonable and prosperous. 'And never,' said he, in conclusion, 'did my delectable little friends serve me so cogently, as in suggesting my stratagem at your sight. If you do not directly name, they squeaked in my ear, her brother and sister, she may demur at accompanying you: if her brother and sister honour your assertion, you will fix the matchless Wanderer in her proper sphere; if they protest against it,—what giant stands in the way to your rearing and protecting the lovely flower yourself?—This was the manner in which these hovering little beings egged me on; but whether, with the playful philanthropy of courteous sylphs, to win me your gentle smiles; or whether, with the wanton malignity of little devils, to annihilate me with your frowns, is still locked up in the womb of your countenance!'

He then farther added, that Riley had accompanied him throughout the expedition; but that, always exhilarated by scenes which excited curiosity, or which produced commotion; he had scampered into the inn, to witness the culprit's being secured, while Sir Jaspar had paid his respects at the chaise.

With a disappointed heart, and with affrighted spirits, Juliet now saw that she must again, and immediately, renew her melancholy flight, in search of a solitary hiding-place; till she could be assured of the positive embarkation of the commissary.

In vain Sir Jaspar pressed to pursue his design of conveying her to her family; the dread of Lord Denmeath, who was in actual communication and league with her persecutor, decided her refusal; though, while she had believed in Sir Jaspar's commission for seeking her, neither risk nor doubt had had power to check the ardour of her impatience, to cast herself upon the protection of Lord Melbury and Lady Aurora: but she felt no courage,—however generously they had succoured and distinguished her as a distressed individual,—to rush upon them, uncalled and unexpected, as a near relation; and one who had so large a claim, could her kindred be proved, upon their inheritance.

Her most earnest wish was to rejoin her Gabriella; but there, where she had been discovered, she could least hope to lie concealed. She must still, therefore, fly, in lonely silence. But she besought Sir Jaspar to take her any whither rather than to Salisbury, where she had had the horrour of being examined by the advertisement.

Proud to receive her commands, he recommended to her a farm-house about three miles from the city, of which the proprietor and his wife, who were worthy and honest people, had belonged, formerly, to his family.

She thankfully agreed to this proposal: but, when they arrived at the farm, they heard that the master and mistress were gone to a neighbouring fair, whence they were not expected back for an hour or two; and that they had locked up the parlour. Some labourers being in the kitchen, Sir Jaspar proposed driving about in the interval; and ordered the postilion to Wilton.

CHAPTER LXXXII

Absorbed in grief, and unable to converse, though endeavouring to listen to the Baronet, Juliet was only drawn from her melancholy reverie, by the rattling of the carriage upon a pavement, as it passed, through a spacious gate, into the court-yard of a magnificent country seat.

She demanded what this meant.

Where better, he demanded in return, could she while away the interval of waiting, than in viewing the finest works of art, displayed in a temple consecrated to their service?

This was a scheme to force back all her consideration. In hearing him pronounce the word Wilton, she had merely thought of the town; not of the mansion of the Earl of Pembroke; which she now positively refused entering; earnestly representing the necessity, as well as propriety, in a situation so perilous, of the most entire obscurity.

He assured her that she would be less liable to observation in a repository of the *beaux arts*, at the villa of a nobleman, than by waiting in a post-chaise, before the door of an inn; as he must indispensably change horses; and grant a little repose to his old groom, who had been out with him all day.

This she could not dispute, convinced, herself, that her greatest danger lay in being recognized, or remarked, within the precincts of an inn.

Nevertheless, how enter into such a mansion in a garb so unfit for admission? She besought him to ask leave that she might remain in some empty apartment, as an humble dependent, while he viewed the house.

Extremely pleased by an idea so consonant to his fantastic taste, he answered her aloud, in alighting, 'Yes, yes, Mrs Betty! if you wish to see the rooms, that you may give an account of all the pretty images to my little ones, there can be no objection.'

She descended from the chaise, meaning to remonstrate upon this misconstruction of her request; but, not allowing her the opportunity, he gaily represented, to the person who shewed him the mansion, that he was convoying a young nursery-maid, the daughter of a worthy old tenant, to his grand-children; and that she had a fancy to see all the finery, that she might make out some pretty stories, to tell the little dears, when she wanted to put them to sleep.

Juliet, whose deep distress made her as little desire to see as to be seen, repeated that she wished to sit still in some spare room: he walked on, pretending not to hear her, addressing himself to his *Cicerone*, whom he kept at his side; and therefore, as there was no female in view, to whom she could apply, she was compelled to follow.

Not as Juliet she followed; Juliet whose soul was delightedly 'awake to tender strokes of art,' whether in painting, music, or poetry; who never saw excellence without emotion; and whose skill and taste would have heightened her pleasure into rapture, her approbation into enthusiasm, in viewing the delicious assemblage of painting, statuary, antiques, natural curiosities, and artificial rarities, of Wilton;—not as Juliet, she followed; but as one to whom every thing was indifferent; whose discernment was gone, whose eyes were dimmed, whose powers of perception were asleep, and whose spirit of enjoyment was annihilated. Figures of the noblest sculpture; busts of historical interest; *alto* and *basso relievos* of antique elegance; marbles, alabasters, spars, and lavers of all colours, and in all forms; pictures glowing into life, and statues appearing to command their beholders;—all that, at another period, would have made her forget every thing but themselves, now vainly solicited a moment of her attention.

It was by no means the fault of the Baronet, that this nearly morbid insensibility was not conquered, by the revivyfying objects which surrounded her. He suffered her not to pass an Æsculapius, without demanding a prescription for her health; a Mercury, without supplicating an ordonnance for her spirits; a Minerva, without claiming an exhortation to courage; nor a Venus, without pointing out, that perpetual beauty beams but through perpetual smiles: couching every phrase under emblematical recommendations of story-subjects for the nursery.

When the guide stood somewhat aloof, 'What say you, now,' he exultingly whispered, 'to my famous little friends? Did they ever devise a more ingenious gambol? From your slave, by a mere wave of their wand, they have transformed me into your master! Ah, wicked syren! a dimple of yours demolishes all their work, and again totters me down to your feet!'

Nevertheless, even in this nearly torpid state, accident having raised her eyes to Vandyke's children of Charles the First, the extraordinary attraction of that fascinating picture, was exciting, unconsciously, some pleasure, when the sound of a carriage announcing a party to see the house, she petitioned Sir Jaspar to avoid, if possible, being known.

All compliance with whatever she could wish, the Baronet promised to nail his eyes to the lowest picture in the room, should they be joined by any stragglers; and then, relinquishing all further examination, he begged permission to wait for his horses, in an apartment which is presided by a noble picture of Salvator Rosa; to which, never discouraged, he strove to call the attention of Juliet.

Nothing could more aptly harmonize, not only with his enthusiastic eulogiums, but with his quaint fancy, than that exquisite effusion of the painter's imagination, 'where, surely,' said the rapturous Baronet, 'his pencil has been guided, if not impelled, in every stroke, by my dear little cronies the fairies! And that variety of vivifying objects; that rich, yet so elegant scenery, of airy gaiety, and ideal felicity, is palpably a representation of fairy land itself! Is it thither my dear little friends will, some day, convey me? And shall I be metamorphosed into one of those youthful swains, that are twining their garlands with such bewitching grace? And shall I myself elect the fair one, around whom I shall entwine mine?'

This harangue was interrupted, by the appearance of a newly arrived party; but vainly Sir Jaspar kept his word, in reclining upon his crutches, till he was nearly prostrate upon the ground; he was immediately challenged by a lady; and that lady was Mrs Ireton.

Juliet, inexpressibly shocked, hastily glided from the room, striving to cover her face with her luxuriously curling hair. She rambled about the mansion, till she met with a chambermaid, from whom she entreated permission to wait in some private apartment, till the carriage to which she belonged should be ready.

The maid, obligingly, took her to a small room; and Juliet, taught by her cruel confusion at the sight of Mrs Ireton, the censure, if not slander, to which travelling alone with a man, however old, might make her liable; determined, at whatever hazard, to hang, henceforth, solely upon herself. She resolved, therefore, to beg the assistance of this maid-servant, to direct her to some safe rural lodging.

But how great was her consternation, when, requiring, now, her purse, she suddenly missed,—what, in her late misery, she had neither guarded nor thought of, her packet and her work-bag!

Every pecuniary resource was now sunk at a blow! even the deposit, which she had held as sacred, of Harleigh, was lost!

At what period of her disturbances this misfortune had happened, she had no knowledge; nor whether her property had been dropt in her distress, or purloined; or simply left at the inn; the consequence, every way, was equally dreadful: and but for Sir Jaspar, whom all sense of propriety had told her, the moment before, to shun, yet to whom, now, she became tied, by absolute necessity, her Difficulties, at this conjuncture, would have been nearly distracting.

When the carriage was returned, with fresh horses, Sir Jaspar found her in a situation of augmented dismay, that filled him with concern; though he also saw, that it was tempered by a grateful softness to himself, that he thought more than ever bewitching.

He assured her that Mrs Ireton, whom he had adroitly shaken off, had not perceived her; but the moment that they were re-seated in the chaise, she communicated to him, with the most painful suffering, the new, and terrible stroke, by which she was oppressed.

Viewing this as a mere pecuniary embarrassment, the joy of becoming again useful, if not necessary, to her, sparkled in his eyes with almost youthful vivacity; though he engaged to send his valet immediately to the inn, to make enquiries, and offer rewards, for recovering the strayed goods.

This second loss of her purse, she suffered Sir Jaspar, without any attempt at justification, to call an active epigram upon modern female drapery; which prefers continual inconvenience, innumerable privations, and the most distressing untidiness, to the antique habit of modesty and good housewifery, which, erst, left the public display of the human figure to the statuary; deeming that to support the female character was more essential than to exhibit the female form.

This second loss, also, by carrying back her reflections to the first, brought to her mind several circumstances, which cast a new light upon that origin of the various misfortunes and adventures which had followed her arrival; and all her recollections, now she knew the rapacity and worthlessness of the pilot, pointed out to her that she had probably been robbed, at the moment when, impulsively, she was pouring forth, upon her knees, her thanks for her deliverance. Her work-bag, which, upon that occasion, she had deposited upon her seat, she remembered, though she had then attributed it to his vigilance and care, seeing in his hands, when she arose.

Arrived at the farm-house, they found themselves expected by the farmer and his wife, who paid the utmost respect to Sir Jaspar; but who saw, with an air of evidently suspicious surprize, the respect which he himself paid to Mrs Betty, the nurse-maid; whose beauty, with her rustic attire, and disordered hair, would have made them instantly conclude her to be a lost young creature, had not the decency of her look, the dignity of her manner, and the grief visible in her countenance, spoken irresistibly in favour of her innocence. They spoke not, however, in favour of that of Sir Jaspar, whose old character of gallantry was well known to them; and induced their belief, that he was inveigling this young woman from her friends, for her moral destruction. They accommodated her, nevertheless, for the night; but, whatever might be their pity, determined, should the Baronet visit her the next day, to invent some other occupation for their spare bedroom.

Unenviable was that night, as passed by their lodger, however acceptable to her was any asylum. She spent it in continual alarm; now shaking with the terrour of pursuit; now affrighted with the prospect of being pennyless; now shocked to find herself cast completely into the power of a man, who, however aged, was her professed admirer; and now distracted by varying resolutions upon the measures which she ought immediately to take. And when, for a few minutes, her eyes, from extreme fatigue, insensibly closed, her dreams, short and horrible, renewed the dreadful event of the preceding day; again she saw herself pursued; again felt herself seized; and she blessed the piercing shrieks with which she awoke, though they brought to her but the transient relief that she was safe for the passing moment.

CHAPTER LXXXIII

Sir Jaspar arrived late the next morning, in wrath, he said, with his valet, who was not yet returned with the result of his enquiries from the inn; but before Juliet could express any uneasiness at the delay, the farmer and his wife, in evident confusion, though with professions of great respect, humbly besought that his honour would excuse their mentioning, that they expected a relation, to pass some days with them, who would want the spare apartment.

The Baronet, however displeased, humourously answered that their relation was mightily welcome to pass his days with them, provided he would be so kind as to go to the neighbouring public-house to take his dreams: but Juliet, much hurt, though with an air of dignity that made her hosts look more abashed than herself, desired that she might not incommode the family; and entreated Sir Jaspar to convey her to the nearest town.

Sir Jaspar, rather to confound than to gratify the farmer, flung down a guinea, which the man vainly sought to decline; and then led the way to the carriage; at the door of which, stopping, he said, with an arch smile, that he was not yet superannuated enough to take place of a fair female; and desired that Mrs Betty would get in first.

Shocked as Juliet felt to find herself thus suspiciously situated, the affront was soon absorbed in the dread of greater evil; in the affright of pursuit, and the dismay of being exposed to improper pecuniary obligations.

Not knowing the country, and not heeding the way that she went, she concluded that they were driving to some neighbouring village, in search of a new lodging; till she perceived that the carriage, which was drawn by four horses, was laboriously mounting a steep acclivity.

Looking then around her, she found herself upon a vast plain; nor house, nor human being, nor tree, nor cattle within view.

Surprised, 'Where are we?' she cried, 'Sir Jaspar? and whither are we going?'

To a quick meeting with his valet, he answered, by a difficult road, rarely passed, because out of the common track.

They then quietly proceeded; Juliet, wrapt up in her own fears and affairs, making no comment upon the looks of enjoyment, and contented taciturnity of her companion; till the groom, riding up to the window, said that the horses could go no further.

Sir Jaspar ordered them a feed; and enquired of Juliet whether she would chuse, while they took a little rest, to mount on foot to the summit of the ascent, and examine whether any horsemen were yet within sight.

Glad to breathe a few minutes alone, she alighted and walked forward; though slowly, and with eyes bent upon the turf; till she was struck by the appearance of a wide ditch between a circular double bank; and perceived that she was approaching the scattered remains of some ancient building, vast, irregular, strange, and in ruins.

Excited by sympathy in what seemed lonely and undone, rather than by curiosity, she now went on more willingly, though not less sadly; till she arrived at a stupendous assemblage of enormous stones, of which the magnitude demanded ocular demonstration to be entitled to credibility. Yet, though each of them, taken separately, might seem, from its astonishing height and breadth, there, like some rock, to have been placed from 'the beginning of things,' and though not even the rudest sculpture denoted any vestige of human art, still the whole was clearly no phenomenon of nature. The form, that might still be traced, of an antique structure, was evidently circular and artificial; and here and there, supported by gigantic posts, or pillars, immense slabs of flat stone were raised horizontally, that could only by manual art and labour have been elevated to such a height. Many were fallen; many, with grim menace, looked nodding; but many, still sustaining their upright direction, were so ponderous that they appeared to have resisted all the wars of the elements, in this high and bleak situation, for ages.

Struck with solemn wonder, Juliet for some time wandered amidst these massy ruins, grand and awful, though terrific rather than attractive. Mounting, then, upon a fragment of the pile, she saw that the view all around was in perfect local harmony with the wild edifice, or rather remains of an edifice, into which she had pierced. She discerned, to a vast extent, a boundless plain, that, like the ocean, seemed to have no term but the horizon; but which, also like the ocean, looked as desert as it was unlimited. Here and there flew a bustard, or a wheat-ear; all else seemed unpeopled air, and uncultivated waste.

In a state of mind so utterly deplorable as that of Juliet, this grand, uncouth monument of ancient days had a certain sad, indefinable attraction, more congenial to her distress, than all the polish, taste, and delicacy of modern skill. The beauties of Wilton seemed appendages of luxury, as well as of refinement; and appeared to require not only sentiment, but happiness for their complete enjoyment: while the nearly savage, however wonderful work of antiquity, in which she was now rambling; placed in this abandoned spot, far from the intercourse, or even view of mankind, with no prospect but of heath and sky; blunted, for the moment, her sensibility, by removing her wide from all the objects with which it was in contact; and insensibly calmed her spirits; though not by dissipating her reverie. Here, on the contrary, was room for 'meditation even to madness;' nothing distracted the sight, nothing broke in upon attention, nor varied the ideas. Thought, uninterrupted and uncontrouled, was master of the mind.

Here, in deep and melancholy rumination, she remained, till she was joined by the Baronet; who toiled after his fair charge with an eager will, though with slack and discourteous feet.

'Do you divine, my beauteous Wanderer,' he cried, 'what part of the globe you now brighten? Have you developed my stratagem to surprize you by a view of what, perhaps, you thought impossible, something curious, and worthy of attention, though more antique than myself?'

Juliet tried, but vainly, to make a civil speech; and Sir Jaspar, after having vainly awaited it, went on.

'You picture yourself, perhaps, in the original temple of Gog and Magog? for what less than giants could have heaved stones such as these? but 'tis not so; and you, who are pious, must view this spot, with bended knees and new ideas. Dart, then, around, the "liquid lustre of those eyes,—so brightly mutable, so sweetly wild!"[12]—and behold in each stony spectre, now staring you in the face, a petrified old Druid! for learn, fair fugitive, you ramble now within the holy precincts of that rude wonder of other days, and disgrace of modern geometry, Stonehenge.'

In almost any other frame of mind, Juliet, from various descriptions, joined to the vicinity of Salisbury, would not have required any nomenclator to have told her where she was: but she could now make no reflections, save upon her own misery; and no combinations, that were not relative to her own dangers.

Sir Jaspar apologized that he had not more roughly handled the farmer and his wife, for their inhospitality; and frankly owned that it was not from the milkiness of his nature that he had been so docile, but from an ardent eagerness to visit Stonehenge with so fair a companion.

Juliet, alarmed, demanded whether he had not taken the route by which they were to meet his valet?

'I have all my life,' continued he, 'fostered, as the wish next my heart, the idea of being the object of some marvellous adventure: but fortune, more deaf, if possible, than blind! has hitherto famished all my elevated desires, by keeping me to the strict regimen of mere common life. Nevertheless, to die like a brute, without leaving behind me one staring anecdote, to be recounted by my successors to my little nephews and nieces;—no! I cannot resolve upon so hum-drum an exit. Late, therefore, last night, I counselled with my tiny friends; and the rogues told me that those whom adventures would not seek, must seek adventures. They then suggested to me, that to visit some romantic spot, far removed from all living ken, or a vast unfrequented plain; where no leering eye, with deriding scrutiny, no envious ear, with prepared impertinence, could peep, or overhear;—where not even a bird could find a twig for the sole of his paw;—there to encounter a lovely nymph; to dally with her in dulcet discourse; to feast upon the sweet notes of her melodious voice;—while obedient fays, and sprightly elves, should accoutre some chosen fragment with offerings appropriate to the place and the occasion—'

One of his grooms, here, demanded of him a private audience.

He retired to some distance, and the heart-oppressed Juliet relieved her struggling feelings by weeping without controul.

While pondering upon her precarious destiny, she perceived, through an opening between two large stones, that Sir Jaspar had placed himself upon an eminence, where, apparently, by his gestures, he was engaged in an animated discourse.

She concluded that the valet de chambre was arrived from the inn; but, soon afterwards, she was struck with motions so extraordinary, and by an appearance of a vivacity so extravagant, that she almost feared the imagination of the Baronet had played him false, and was superseding his reason. She arose, and softly approaching, endeavoured to discover with whom he was conversing; but could discern no one, and was the more alarmed; though the nearer she advanced, the less he seemed to be an object of pity; his countenance being as bright with glee, as his hands and arms were busy with action.

After some time, she caught his eye; when, ceasing all gesticulation, he kissed his hand, with a motion that invited her approach; and, gallantly resigning his seat, begged her permission to take one by her side.

He was all smiling good humour; and his features, in defiance of his age, expressed the most playful archness. 'It is not,' he cried, 'for nothing, permit me to assure you, that I have prowled over this druidical spot; for though the Druids have not been so debonnaire as to re-animate themselves to address me, they have suffered a flat surface of their petrifaction to be covered over with a whole army of my little frequenters; who have dragged thither a parcel, and the Lord knows what besides, that they have displayed, as you see, full before me; after which, with their usual familiarity, up they have been mounting to my shoulders, my throat, my ears, and my wig; and lolling all about me, in mockery of my remonstrances; saying, Harkee, old Sir!—for they use very little ceremony with me;—didst thou really fancy we would suffer the loveliest lily of the valley to droop without any gentle shade, under the blazing glare of this full light, while thy aukward clown of a valet trots to the inn for her bonnet? or let her wait his plodding return, for what other drapery her fair form may require? or permit her to be famished in the open air, whilst thou art hopping and hobbling, and hobbling and hopping, about these ruins, which thou art so fast ossifying to resemble? No, old Sir! look what our wands have brought hither for her! look!—but touch nothing for thy life! her own lily hands alone must develop our fairy gifts.'

Juliet, who, already, had observed, upon the nearest flat stone, a large band-box, and a square new trunk, placed as supporters to an elegant Japan basket, in which were arranged various refreshments; could not, however disconcerted by attentions that she knew not how to acknowledge, prevail upon herself to damp the exaltation of his spirits, by resisting his entreaty that she would herself lift up the lid of the trunk and open the band-box.

The first of these machines presented to her sight a complete small assortment of the finest linen; the second contained a white chip bonnet of the most beautiful texture.

This last excited a transient feeling of pleasure, in offering some shade for her face, now exposed to every eye. She looked at it, wistfully, a few minutes, anticipating its umbrageous succour; yet irresolute, and fearing to give encouragement to the too evident admiration of the Baronet. Her deliberation, nevertheless, seconded by her wishes, was in his favour. She passed over, in her mind, that he knew her origin, and high natural, however disputed expectations; and that, with all his gallantry, he was not only aged and sickly, but a gentleman in manners and sentiments, as much as in birth and rank of life. He could not mean her dishonour; and to shew, since thus cast into his hands, and loaded with obligations of long standing, as well as recent, a voluntary confidence in his character and intentions, might, happily, from mingling a sense of honour with a sense of shame, turn aside what was wrong in his regard, and give pride and pleasure to a nobler attachment, that might fix him her solid and disinterested friend for life.

Decided by this view of things, she thankfully consented to receive his offerings, upon condition that he would permit her to consider him as the banker of Lord Melbury and of Lady Aurora Granville.

Enchanted by her acceptance, and enraptured by its manner, the first sensation of the melted Baronet was to cast himself at her feet: but the movement was checked by certain aches and pains; while the necessity of picking up one of his crutches, which, in his transport, had fallen from his hands, mournfully called him back from his gallantry to his infirmities.

At this moment, an 'Ah ha! here's the Demoiselle!—Here she is, faith!' suddenly presented before them Riley, mounted upon a fragment of the pile, to take a view around him.

Starting, and in dread of some new horrour, Juliet looked at him aghast; while, clapping his hands, and turbently approaching her, he exclaimed, 'Yes! here she is, *in propria persona*! I was afraid that she had slipped through our fingers again! Monsieur *le cher Epoux* will have a pretty tight job of it to get her into conjugal trammels! he will, faith!'

To the other, and yet more horrible sensations of Juliet, this speech added a depth of shame nearly overwhelming, from the implied obloquy hanging upon the character of a wife eloping from her husband.

Presently, however, all within was changed; re-invigourated, new strung! and joy, irresistibly, beamed from her eyes, and hope glowed upon her cheeks, as Riley related that, before he had left the inn upon the road, he had himself seen the new Mounseer, with poor Surly, who had been seized as an accomplice, packed off together for the sea-coast, whence they were both, with all speed, to be embarked for their own dear country.

The Baronet waved his hand, in act of congratulation to Juliet, but forbore speaking; and Riley went on.

'They made confounded wry faces, and grimaces, both of them. I never saw a grimmer couple! They amused me mightily; they did, faith! But I can't compliment you, Demoiselle, upon your choice of a loving partner. He has as hang-dog a physiognomy as a Bow Street prowler might wish to light upon on a summer's day. A most fiend-like aspect, I confess. I don't well make out what you took to him for, Demoiselle? His Cupid's arrows must have been handsomely tipt with gold, to blind you to all that brass of his brow and his port.'

Sir Jaspar, distressed for Juliet, and much annoyed by this interruption, however happy in the intelligence to which it was the vehicle, enquired what chance had brought Mr Riley to Stonehenge?

The chance, he answered, that generally ruled his actions, namely, his own will and pleasure. He had found out, in his prowls about Salisbury, that Sir Jaspar was to be followed to Stonehenge by a dainty repast; and, deeming his news well worth a bumper to the loving sea-voyagers, he had borrowed a horse of one of Master Baronet's grooms, to take his share in the feast.

The Baronet, at this hint, instantly, and with scrupulous politeness, did the honours of his stores; though he was ready to gnash his teeth with ire, at so mundane an appropriation of his fairy purposes.

'What a rare hand you are, Demoiselle,' cried Riley, 'at hocus pocus work! Who the deuce, with that Hebe face of yours, could have thought of your being a married woman! Why, when I saw you at the old Bang'em's concert, at Brighthelmstone, I should have taken you for a boarding-school Miss. But you metamorphose yourself about so, one does not know which way to look for you. Ovid was a mere fool to you. His nymphs, turned into trees, and rivers, and flowers, and beasts, and fishes, make such a staring chaos of lies, that one reads them without a ray of reference to truth; like the tales of the Genii, or of old Mother Goose. He makes such a comical hodge podge of animal, vegetable, and mineral choppings and changes, that we should shout over them, as our brats do at a puppet-shew, when old Nick teaches punchinello the devil's dance down to hell; or pummels his wife to a mummy; if it were not for the sly rogue's tickling one's ears so cajolingly with the jingle of metre. But Demoiselle, here, scorns all that namby pamby work.'

Sir Jaspar tried vainly to call him to order; the embarrassment of Juliet operated but as a stimulus to his caustic humour.

'I have met with nothing like her, Master Baronet,' he continued, 'all the globe over. Neither juggler nor conjuror is a match for her. She can make herself as ugly as a witch, and as handsome as an angel. She'll answer what one only murmurs in a whisper; and she won't hear a word, when one bawls as loud as a speaking-trumpet. Now she turns herself into a vagrant, not worth sixpence; and now, into a fine player and singer that ravishes all ears, and might make, if it suited her fancy, a thousand pounds at her benefit: and now, again, as you see, you can't tell whether she's a house-maid, or a country girl! yet a devilish fine creature, faith! as fine a creature as ever I beheld,—when she's in that humour! Look but what a beautiful head of hair she's displaying to us now! It becomes her mightily. But I won't swear that she does not change it, in a minute or two, for a skull-cap! She's a droll girl, faith! I like her prodigiously!'

Utterly disconcerted, Juliet, expressively bowing to the Baronet, lifted up the lid of the band-box, and, encircling her head in his bonnet, begged his permission to re-seat herself in the chaise.

Charmed with the prospect of another tête à tête, Sir Jaspar, with alacrity, accompanied her to the carriage; leaving Riley to enjoy, at his leisure, the cynical satisfaction, of having worried a timid deer from the field.

Still, however, Juliet, while uncertain whether the embarkation might not be eluded, desired to adhere to her plan of privacy and obscurity; and the Baronet would not struggle against a resolution from which he hoped to reap the fruit of lengthened intercourse. Pleased and willingly, therefore, he told his postilion to drive across the plain to ———, whence they proceeded post to Blandford.

Great was the relief afforded to the feelings of Juliet, by a removal so expeditious from the immediate vicinity of the scene of her sufferings; but she considered it, at the same time, to be a circumstance to obviate all necessity, and, consequently, all propriety of further attendance from the Baronet: here, therefore, to his utter dismay, with firmness, though with the gentlest acknowledgements, she begged that they might separate.

Cruelly disappointed, Sir Jaspar warmly remonstrated against the danger of her being left alone; but the possible hazards which might be annexed to acting right, could not deter her from the certain evil of acting wrong. Her greatest repugnance was that of being again forced to accept pecuniary aid; yet that, which, however disagreeable, might be refunded, was at least preferable to the increase and continuance of obligations, which, besides their perilous tendency, could never be repaid. Already, upon opening the band-box, she had seen a well furnished purse; and though her first movement had prompted its rejection, the decision of necessity was that of acceptance.

When Sir Jaspar found it utterly impossible to prevail with his fair companion still to bear that title, he expostulated against leaving her, at least, in a public town; and she was not sorry to accept his offer of conveying her to some neighbouring village.

It was still day-light, when they arrived within the picturesque view of a villa, which Juliet, upon enquiry, heard was Milton-abbey. She soon discovered, that the scheme of the Baronet, to lengthen their sojourn with each other, was to carry her to see the house: but this she absolutely refused; and her seriousness compelled him to drive to a neighbouring cottage; where she had the good fortune to meet with a clean elderly woman, who was able to accommodate her with a small chamber.

Here, not without sincere concern, she saw the reluctance, even to sadness, with which her old admirer felt himself forced to leave his too lovely young friend: and what she owed to him was so important, so momentous, that she parted from him, herself, with real regret, and with expressions of the most lively esteem and regard.

CHAPTER LXXXIV

Restless, again, was the night of Juliet; bewildered with varying visions of hope, of despair, of bliss, of horrour; now presenting a fair prospect that opened sweetly to her best affections; now shewing every blossom blighted, by a dark, overwhelming storm.

To engage the good will of her new hostess, she bestowed upon her nearly every thing that she had worn upon entering the cottage. What she had been seen and discovered in, could no longer serve any purpose of concealment; and all disguise was disgusting to her, if not induced by the most imperious necessity. She clothed herself, therefore, from the fairy stores of her munificent old sylph; with whom her debts were so multiplied and so considerable, that she meant, at all events, to call upon her family for their disbursement.

The quietness of this residence, induced her to propose remaining here: and her new hostess, who was one of the many who, where interest preaches passiveness, make it a point not to be troublesome, consented, without objection or enquiry.

Hence, again, she wrote to Gabriella, from whom she languished for intelligence.

In this perfect retirement, she passed her time in deep rumination; her thoughts for ever hovering around the Bishop, upon whose fate her own invariably depended.

Her little apartment was close and hot; unshaded by blinds, unsheltered by shutters; she went forth, therefore, early every morning, to enjoy fresh air in the cool of a neighbouring wood, which, once having entered, she knew not how to quit. Solitude there, had not the character of seclusion; it bore not, as in her room, the air of banishment, if not of imprisonment; and the beautiful prospects around her, though her sole, were a never-failing source of recreation.

She permitted not, however, her love of the country to beguile her into danger by the love of variety; she wandered not far from her new habitation, in the vicinity of Milton-abbey; of which she never lost sight from distance, though frequently from intervening hills and trees.

But no answer arrived from Gabriella; and, in a few days, her own letter was returned, with a line written by the post-man upon the cover, to say, No. — Frith-street, Soho, was empty.

New sorrow, now, and fearful distress assailed every feeling of Juliet: What could have occasioned this sudden measure? Whither was Gabriella gone? Might it be happiness?—or was it some new evil that had caused this change of abode? The letter sent to Salisbury had never been claimed; nor did Juliet dare demand it: but Gabriella might, perhaps, have written her new plan by the address sent from the farm-house.

It was now that she blessed the munificent Sir Jaspar, to whose purse she had immediate recourse for sending a man and horse to the cottage; with written instructions to enquire for a letter, concerning which she had left directions with the good old cottager.

While, to wear away the hours devoted to anxious waiting, she wandered, as usual, in the view of Milton-abbey, from a rich valley, bounded by rising hills, whose circling slopes bore the form of undulating waves, she perceived, from a small distance, a horseman galloping towards her cottage.

It could not already be her messenger. She felt uneasy, and, gliding to the brow of an eminence, sat down upon the turf, as much as possible out of sight.

In a short time, she heard the quick pacing step of a man in haste. She tried to place herself still more obscurely; but, by moving, caught the eye of the object she meant to avoid. He approached her rapidly, but when near enough to distinguish her, abruptly stopt, as if to recollect himself; and Juliet, at the same moment that she was herself discerned, recognized Harleigh.

With difficulty restraining an exclamation, from surprize and painful emotion, she looked round to discover if it would be possible to elude him; but she could only walk towards Milton-abbey, in full view herself from that noble seat; or immediately face him by returning to her home. She stood still, therefore, though bending her eye to the ground; hurt and offended that, at such a juncture, Harleigh could break into her retreat; and grieved yet more deeply, that Harleigh could excite in her even transitory displeasure.

Harleigh stept forward, but his voice, husky and nervous, so inarticulately pronounced something relative to a packet and a work-bag, that Juliet, losing her displeasure in a sudden hope of hearing some news of her property, raised her head, with a look that demanded an explanation.

Still he strove in vain for sufficient calmness to speak distinctly; yet his answer gave Juliet to understand, that he had conveyed her packet and work-bag to the cottage which he had been told she inhabited.

'And where, Sir,' cried Juliet, surprized into vivacity and pleasure at this unexpected hearing, 'how, and where have they been recovered?'

Harleigh now blushed himself, at the blushes which he knew he must raise in her cheeks, as he replied, that the packet and the work-bag which he had brought, had been dropt in his room at the inn.

Crimson is pale to the depth of red with which shame and confusion dyed her face; while Harleigh, recovering his voice, sought to relieve her embarrassment, by more rapidly continuing his discourse.

'I should sooner have endeavoured to deliver these articles, but that I knew not, till yesterday, that they had fallen to my care. I had left the inn, to follow, and seek Sir Jaspar Herrington; but having various papers and letters in my room, that I had not had time to collect, I obtained leave to take away the key with me, of the landlady, to whom I was well known,—for there, or in that neighbourhood, an irresistible interest has kept me, from the time that, through my groom, I had heard … who had been seen … at Bagshot … entering the Salisbury stage!—Yesterday, when I returned, to the inn, I first perceived these parcels.'—

He stopt; but Juliet could not speak, could not look up; could pronounce no apology, nor enter into any explanation.

'Sir Jaspar Herrington,' he continued, 'whom I have just left, is still at Salisbury; but setting out for town. From him I learnt your immediate direction; but not knowing what might be the value of the packets, nor,—' He hesitated a moment, and then, with a sigh, added, 'nor how to direct them! I determined upon venturing to deliver them myself.'

The tingling cheeks of Juliet, at the inference of the words 'nor how to direct them,' seemed on fire; but she was totally silent.

'I have carefully sealed them,' he resumed, 'and I have delivered them to the woman of the cottage, for the young lady who at present sleeps there; and, hearing that that young lady was walking in the neighbourhood, I ventured to follow, with this intelligence.'

'You are very good, Sir,' Juliet strove to answer; but her lips were parched, and no words could find their way.

This excess of timidity brought back the courage of Harleigh, who, advancing a step or two, said, 'You will not be angry that Sir Jaspar, moved by my uncontrollable urgency, has had the charity to reveal to me some particulars….'

'Oh! make way for me to pass, Mr Harleigh!' now interrupted Juliet, forcing her voice, and striving to force a passage.

'Did you wish, then,' said Harleigh, in a tone the most melancholy, 'could you wish that I should still languish in harrowing suspense? or burst with ignorance?'

'Oh no!' cried she, raising her eyes, which glistened with tears, 'no! If the mystery that so long has hung about me, by occupying your ...' She sought a word, and then continued: 'your imagination ... impedes the oblivion that ought to bury me and my misfortunes from further thought,—then, indeed, I ought to be thankful to Sir Jaspar,—and I am thankful that he has let you know, ... that he has informed you....'

She could not finish the sentence.

'Yes!' cried Harleigh with energy, 'I have heard the dreadful history of your wrongs! of the violences by which you have suffered, of the inhuman attempts upon your liberty, your safety, your honour!—But since you have thus happily—'

'Mr Harleigh,' cried Juliet, struggling to recover her presence of mind, 'I need no longer, I trust, now, beg your absence! All I can have to say you must, now, understand ... anticipate ... acknowledge ... since you are aware....'

'Ah!' cried Harleigh, in a tone not quite free from reproach;—'had you but, from the beginning, condescended to inform me of your situation! a situation so impossible to divine! so replete with horrour, with injury, with unheard of suffering,—had you, from the first, instead of avoiding, flying me, deigned to treat me with some trust—'

'Mr Harleigh,' said Juliet, with eagerness, 'whatever may be your surprize that such should be my situation, ... my fate, ... you can, at least, require, now, no explanation why I have fled you!'

The word why, vibrated instantly to the heart of Harleigh, where it condolingly said: It was duty, then, not averseness, not indifference, that urged that flight! she had not fled, had she not deemed herself engaged!— Juliet, who had hastily uttered the why in the solicitude of self-vindication, shewed, by a change of complexion, the moment that it had passed her lips, that she felt the possible inference of which it was susceptible, and dropt her eyes; fearful to risk discovering the consciousness that they might indicate.

Harleigh, however, now brightened, glowed with revived sensations: 'Ah! be not,' he cried, 'be not the victim of your scruples! let not your too delicate fears of doing wrong by others, urge you to inflict wrong, irreparable wrong, upon yourself! Your real dangers are past; none now remain but from a fancied,—pardon, pardon me!—a fancied refinement, unfounded in reason, or in right! Suffer, therefore—'

'Hold, Sir, hold!—we must not even talk upon this subject:—nor, at this moment, upon any other!—'

Her brow shewed rising displeasure; but Harleigh was intractable. 'Pronounce not,' he cried, 'an interdiction! I make no claim, no plea, no condition. I will speak wholly as an impartial man;—and have you not condescended to tell me, that as a friend, if to that title,—so limited, yet so honourable,—I would confine myself,—you would not disdain to consult with me? As such, I am now here. I feel, I respect, I revere the delicacy of all your ideas, the perfection of your conduct! I will put, therefore, aside, all that relates not simply to yourself, and to your position; I will speak to you, for the moment, and in his absence,—as—as Lord Melbury!—as your brother!—'

An involuntary smile here unbent the knitting brow of Juliet, who could not feel offended, or sorry, that Sir Jaspar had revealed the history of her birth.

She desired, nevertheless, to pass, refusing every species of discussion.

'If you will not answer, will not speak,' cried Harleigh, still obstructing her way, 'fear not, at least, to hear! Are you not at liberty? Is not your persecutor gone?—Can he ever return?'

'Gone?' repeated Juliet.

'I have myself seen him embark! I rode after his chaise, I pursued it to the sea-coast, I saw him under sail.'

Juliet, with uplifted eyes, clasped her hands, from an emotion of ungovernable joy; which a thousand blushes betrayed her vain struggles to suppress.

Harleigh observed not this unmoved: 'Ah, Madam!' he cried, 'since, thus critically, you have escaped;—since, thus happily, you are released;—since no church ritual has ever sanctioned the sacrilegious violence—'

'Spare all ineffectual controversy!' cried Juliet, assuming an air and tone of composure, with which her quick heaving bosom was ill in harmony; 'I can neither talk nor listen upon this subject. You know, now, my story: dread and atrocious as is my connection, my faith to it must be unbroken, till I have seen the Bishop! and till the iniquity of my chains may be proved, and my restoration to my violated freedom may be legalized. Do not look so shocked; so angry, must I say?—Remember, that a point of conscience can be settled only internally! I will speak, therefore, but one word more; and I must hear no reply: little as I feel to belong to the person in question, I cannot consider myself to be my own! 'Tis a tie which, whether or not it binds me to him, excludes me, while thus circumstanced, from all others!—This, Sir, is my last word!—Adieu!'

Harleigh, though looking nearly petrified, still stood before her. 'You fly us, then,' he cried, resentfully, though mournfully, 'both alike? You put us upon a par?—'

'No!' answered Juliet, hastily, 'him I fly because I hate;—You—'

The deep scarlet which mounted into her whole face finished the sentence; in defiance of a sudden and abrupt breaking off, that meant and hoped to snatch the unguarded phrase from comprehension.

But Harleigh felt its fullest contrast; his hopes, his wishes, his whole soul completed it by You, because I love!—not that he could persuade himself that Juliet would have used those words; he knew the contrary; knew that she would sooner thus situated expire; but such, he felt, was the impulse of her thoughts; such the consciousness that broke off her speech.

He durst not venture at any acknowledgement; but, once appeased in his doubts, and satisfied in his feelings, he respected her opinions, and, yielding to her increased, yet speechless eagerness to be gone, he silently, but with eyes of expressive tenderness, ceased to obstruct her passage.

Utterly confounded herself, at the half-pronounced thought, thus inadvertently surprised from her, and thus palpably seized and interpreted, she strove to devize some term that might obviate dangerous consequences; but she felt her cheeks so hot, so cold, and again so hot, that she durst not trust her face to his observation; and, accepting the opening which he made for her, she was returning to her cottage, tortured,—and yet soothed,—by indescribable emotions; when an energetic cry of 'Ellis!—Harleigh!—Ellis!' made her raise her eyes to the adjacent hill, and perceive Elinor.

CHAPTER LXXXV

With arms extended, and a commanding air, Elinor, having made signs to the dismayed Harleigh not to move, awaited, where she stood, the terrified, but obedient Juliet.

'Avoid me not!' she cried, 'Ellis! why should you avoid me? I have given you back your plighted word; and the pride of Harleigh has saved him from all bonds. Why, then, should you fly?'

Juliet attempted not to make any answer.

'The conference, the last conference,' continued Elinor, 'which so ardently I have demanded, is still unaccorded. Repeatedly I could have surprized it, singly, from Harleigh; but—'

She stopt, coloured, looked indignant, yet ashamed, and then haughtily went on: 'Imagine not my courage tarnished by cowardly apprehensions of misinterpretation,—suspicion,—censoriousness;... no! let the world sneer at its pleasure! Its spleen will never keep pace with my contempt. But Harleigh! —I brave not the censure of Harleigh! even though prepared, and resolved, to quit him for evermore! And, with ideas punctilious such as his of feminine delicacy, he might blame, perhaps,—should I seek him alone—'

She blushed more deeply, and, with extreme agitation, added, 'Harleigh, when we shall meet no more, will always honourably say, Her passion for me might be tinctured with madness, but its purity was without alloy!'

She now turned away, to hide a starting tear; but, soon resuming her usually lively manner, said, 'I have traced you, at last, together; and by means of our caustick, bilious fellow-traveller, Riley; whom I encountered by accident; and who runs, snarling, yet curious, after his fellow-creatures, working at making himself enemies, as if enmity were a pleasing, or lucrative profession! From him I learnt, that he had just seen you,—and together!—near Salisbury. I discovered you, Ellis, two days ago; but Harleigh, though I have been roving some time in your vicinity, only this moment.'

A sudden shriek now broke from her, and Juliet, affrighted and looking around, perceived Harleigh pacing hastily away.

The shriek reached him, and he stopt.

'Fly, fly, to him,' she cried, 'Ellis; assure him, I have no present personal project; none! I solemnly promise, none! But I have an opinion to gather from him, of which my ignorance burns, devours me, and will not let me rest, alive nor dead!'

Juliet, distressed, irresolute, ventured not to move.

''Tis his duty,' continued Elinor, 'after his solemn declaration, to initiate me into his motives for believing in a future state. I have been distracting my burthened senses over theological works; but my head is in no condition to comprehend them. They treat, also, of belief in a future state, as of a thing not to be proved, but to be taken for granted. Let him penetrate me with his own notions; or frankly acknowledge their insufficiency. But let him mark that they are indeed his own! Let them be neither fanatical, illusory, nor traditional.'

Juliet was compelled to obey; but while she was repeating her message, Elinor descended the hill, and they all met at its foot.

'Harleigh,' she cried, 'fear me not! Do not imagine I shall again go over the same ground;—at least, not with the monotonous stupidity of again going over it in the same manner. Yet believe not my resolution to be shaken! But I have some doubts, relative to your own principles and opinions, of which I demand a solution.'

She then seated herself upon the turf, and made Harleigh seat himself before her, while Juliet remained by her side.

'Can you feign, Harleigh? Can you endure to act a part, in defiance of your nobler nature, merely to prolong my detested life? Do you join in the popular cry against suicide, merely to arrest my impatient hand? If not, initiate me, I beseech, in the series of pretended reasoning, by which honour, honesty, and understanding such as yours, have been duped into bigotry? How is it, explain! that you can have been worked upon to believe in an existence after death? Ah, Harleigh! could you, indeed, give so sublime a resting-place to my labouring ideas!—I would consent to enter the ecclesiastical court myself, to sing the recantation of what you deem my errours. And then, Albert, I might learn,—with all my wretchedness!—to bear to live,—for then, I might seek and foster some hope in dying!'

'Dear Elinor!' cried Harleigh, gently, almost tenderly, 'let me send for some divine!'

'How conscious is this retreat,' she cried, 'of the weakness of your cause! Ah! why thus try to bewilder a poor forlorn traveller, who is dropping with fatigue upon her road? and to fret and goad her on, when the poor tortured wretch languishes to give up the journey altogether? Why not rather, more generously, more like yourself, aid her to attain repose? to open her burning veins, and bid her pent up blood flow freely to her relief? or kindly point the steel to her agonized heart, whose last sigh would be ecstacy if it owed its liberation to your pitying hand! Oh Harleigh! what vain prejudice, what superstitious sophistry, robs me of the only solace that could soothe my parting breath?'

'What is it Elinor means?' cried Harleigh, alarmed, yet affecting to speak lightly: 'Has she no compunction for the labour she causes my blood in thus perpetually accelerating its circulation.'

'Pardon me, dear Harleigh, I have inadvertently run from my purpose to my wishes. To the point, then. Make me, if it be possible, conceive how your reason has thus been played upon, and your discernment been set asleep. I have studied this matter abroad, with the ablest casuists, I have met with; and though I may not retain, or detail their reasoning, well enough to make a convert of any other, they have fixed for ever in my own mind, a conviction that death and annihilation are one. Why do you knit your brow?—And see how Ellis starts!—And why do you both look at me as if I were mad? Mad? because I would rather crush misery than endure it? Mad? because I would rather, at my own time, die the death of reason, than by compulsion, and when least disposed, that of nature? Of reason, that appreciates life but by enjoyment; not of nature, that would make misery linger, till malady or old age dissolve the worn out fabric. To indulge our little miserable fears and propensities, we give flattering epithets to all our meannesses; for what is endurance of worldly pain and affliction but folly? what patience, but insipidity? what suffering, but cowardice? Oh suicide! triumphant antidote to woe! straight forward, unerring route to rest, to repose! I call upon thy aid! I invoke—'

'Repose?—rest?' interrupted Harleigh, 'how earned? By deserting our duties? By quitting our posts? By forsaking and wounding all by whom we are cherished?'

'One word, Harleigh, answers all that: Did we ask for our being? Why was it given us if doomed to be wretched? To whom are we accountable for renouncing a donation, made without our consent or knowledge? O, if ever that wretched thing called life has a noble moment, it must surely be that of its voluntary sacrifice! lopping off, at a blow, that hydra-headed monster of evil upon evil, called time; bounding over the imps of superstition; dancing upon the pangs of disease; and boldly, hardily mocking the senseless legends, that would frighten us with eternity!—Eternity? to poor, little, frail, finite beings like us! Oh Albert! worldly considerations, monkish inventions, and superstitious reveries set apart;—reason called forth, truth developed, probabilities canvassed,—say! is it not clear that death is an end to all? an abyss eternal? a conclusion? Nature comes but for succession; though the pride of man would give her resurrection. Mouldering all together we go, to form new earth for burying our successors.'

'Horrible, Elinor, most horrible! yet if, indeed, it is your opinion that you are doomed to sink to nothing; if your soul, in the full tide of its energies, and in the pride of intellect, seems to you a mere appendant to the body; if you believe it to be of the same fragile materials; how can you wish to shorten the so short period of consciousness? to abridge the so brief moment of sensibility? Is it not always time enough to think, feel, see, hear,—love and be loved no more?'

'Yes! 'tis always too soon to lose happiness; but misery,—ah Albert!—why should misery, when it can so easily be stilled, be endured?'

'Stilled, Elinor?—What mean you? By annihilation?—How an infidel assumes fortitude to wish for death, is my constant astonishment! To believe in the eternal loss of all he holds, or knows, or feels; to be persuaded that "this sensible, warm being" will "melt, thaw, and resolve itself into a dew,"—and to believe that there all ends! Surely every species of existence must be preferable to such an expectation from its cessation! Dust! literal dust!—Food for worms!—to be trod upon;—crushed;—dug up;—battered down;—is that our termination? That,—and nothing more?'

''Tis shocking, Albert, no doubt; shocking and disgusting. Yet why disguise the fact? Reason, philosophy, analogy, all prove our materialism. Even common observation, even daily experience, in viewing our natural end, where neither sickness nor accident impede, nor shorten its progress, prove it by superannuation; shew clearly that mind and body, when they die the long death of nature, gradually decline together.'

'Were that double decay constant, Elinor, in its junction, you might thence, perhaps, draw that inference; but does not the body wither as completely by decay, in the very prime, and pride, and bloom of youth, where the death is consumption, as in the most worn-out decrepitude of age? Yet the capacity is often, even to the last minute, as perfect as in the vigour of health. Were all within, as well as all without, material, would not the blight to one involve, uniformly, the blight to the other? How often, too, does age, even the oldest, escape any previous decay of intellect! There are records extant, of those who, after attaining their hundredth year, have been capable of bearing testimony in trials; but are there any of those, who, at half that age, have preserved their external appearance? No. It is the body, therefore, not the soul, that, in a natural state, and free from the accelerations of accident, seems first to degenerate. The grace of symmetry, the charm of expression, may last with our existence, and delight to its latest date; but that which we understand exclusively, as personal perfections,—how soon is it over! Not only before the intellects are impaired, but even, and not rarely, before they are arrived at their full completion. Can mind, then, and body be but one and the same thing, when they neither flourish nor wither together?'

'Ah, Harleigh! is it not your willing mind, that here frames its sentiments from its exaltation? Not your deeper understanding, that defines your future expectations from your rational belief?'

'No, Elinor; my belief in the immortality of the soul may be strengthened, but it is not framed by my wishes. Let me, however, ask you a question in return. Your disbelief of the immortality of the soul, is founded on your inability to have it, visually, or orally, demonstrated: Let me, then, ask, can the nature, use, and destinations of the soul, however darkly hidden from our analysing powers, be more impervious to our limited foresight, than the narrower, yet equally, to us, invisible, destiny of our days to come upon earth? But does any one, therefore, from not knowing its purposes, disbelieve that his life may be lengthened? Yet which of us can divine what his fate will be from year to year? What his actions, from hour to hour? his thoughts, from moment to moment?'

'Oh Harleigh! how fatally is that true! how little did I foresee, when I so delighted in your society, that that very delight would but impel me to burn for the moment of bidding you an eternal farewell!'

Harleigh sighed; but with earnestness continued: 'We conceive the soul to influence, if not to direct our whole construction, yet we have no sensible proof of its being in any part of it: how, then, shall we determine that to be destroyed or departed, which we have never known to be created? never seen to exist? O bow we down! for all is inexplicable! We can but say, the body is obvious in its perfection, and still obvious in its decay; the soul is always unsearchable! were we sure it were only our understanding, we might, perhaps, develop it; or only our feelings, we might catch it; but it is something indefinable, of which the consciousness tells us not the qualities, nor the possession the attributes; and of which the end leaves no trace! We follow it not to its dissolution like the body; which, after what we call death, is still as evident, as when our conception of what is soul were yet lent to it: if the soul, then, be equally material, say, is it still there also? though as unseen and hidden as when breath and motion were yet perceptible?'

'Body and soul, Albert, come together with existence, and together are nullified by death.'

'And are you, Elinor, aware whither such reasoning may lead? If the body instead of being the tenement of the soul, is but one and the same with it;— how are you certain, if they are not sundered by death, that they do not in death, though by means, and with effects to us unknown, still exist together? That with the body, whether animated or inert, the soul may not always be adherent? who shall assure you, who, at least, shall demonstrate, that if the soul be but a part of the body, it may not think, though no utterance can be given to its thoughts; and may not feel, though all expression is at an end, and motion is no more? Whither may such reasoning lead? to what strange suggestions may it not conduct us? to what vain fantasies, what useless horrours? May we not apprehend that the insects, the worms which are formed from the human frame, may partake of and retain human consciousness? May we not imagine those wretched reptiles, which creep from our remains, to be sensible of their fallen state, and tortured by their degradation? to resent, as well as seek to elude the ill usage, the blows, the oppressions to which they are exposed?—'

'Fie! Albert, fie!'

'Nay, what proof, if for proof you wait, have you to the contrary? Is it their writhing? their sensitive shrink from your touch? their agonizing efforts to save their miserable existence from your gripe?'

'Harleigh! Harleigh!'

'And this dust, Elinor, to which you settle that, finally, all will be mouldered or crumbled;—fear you not that its every particle may possess some sensitive quality? When we cease to speak, to move, to breathe, you assert the soul to be annihilated: But why? Is it only because you lose sight of its operations? In chemistry are there not sundry substances which, by certain processes, become invisible, and are sought in vain by the spectator; but which, by other processes, are again brought to view? And shall the chemist have this faculty to produce, and to withdraw, from our sight, and the Creator of All be denied any occult powers?'

'Nay, Albert, "how can we reason but from what we know?"—Will you compare a fact which experiment can prove, which reason may discuss, and which the senses may witness, with a bare possibility? A vague conjecture?'

'Is nothing, then, credible, Elinor, that is out of the province of demonstration? nothing probable, that surpasses our understanding?—nothing sacred that is beyond our view? Are we so perfect in our knowledge, even of what we behold, or possess, as to draw such presumptuous conclusions, of the self-sufficiency and omnipotence of our faculties, for judging what is every way out of our sight, or reach? Do we know one radical point of our existence, here, where "we live, and move, and have our being?" Do we comprehend, unequivocally, our immediate attributes and powers? Can we tell even how our hands obey our will? how our desires suffice to guide our feet from place to place? to roll our eyes from object to object? If all were clear, save the existence and the extinction of the soul, then, indeed, we might pronounce all faith, but in self-evidence, to be folly!'

'Faith! Harleigh, faith? the very word scents of monkish subtleties! 'Tis to faith, to that absurd idea of lulling to sleep our reason, of setting aside our senses, our observation, our knowledge; and giving our ignorant, unmeaning trust, and blind confidence to religious quacks; 'tis to that, precisely that, you owe what you term our infidelity; for 'tis that which has provoked the spirit of investigation, which has shewn us the pusillanimity and imbecility of consigning the short period in which we possess our poor fleeting existence, to other men's uses, deliberations, schemes, fancies, and ordinances. For what else can you call submission to unproved assertions, and concurrence in unfounded belief?'

'And yet, this faith, Elinor, which, in religion, you renounce, despise, or defy, because in religion you would think, feel, and believe by demonstration alone, you insensibly admit in nearly all things else! Have you it not in morals? Does society exist but by faith? Does friendship,—I will not name what is so open to controversy as love,—but say! has friendship any other tie? has honour any other bond than faith? We have no proofs, no demonstrations of worth that can reach the regions of the heart: we judge but by effects; we believe but by analogies; we love, we esteem, we trust but by credulity, by faith! For where is the mathematician who can calculate what may be pronounced of the mind, from what is seen in the countenance, or uttered by speech? yet is any one therefore so wretched, as not to feel any social reliance beyond what he can mathematically demonstrate to be merited?'

'And to what but that, Albert, precisely that, do we owe being so perpetually duped and betrayed? to what but building upon false trust? upon appearance, and not certainty?'

'Certainty, Elinor! Where, and in what is certainty to be found? If you disclaim belief in immortality upon faith, as insufficient to satisfy reason, what is the basis even of your disbelief? Is it not faith also? When you demand the proofs of immortality, let me demand, in return, what are your proofs of materialism? And, till you can bring to demonstration the operations of the soul while we live, presume not to decide upon its extinction when we die! Of the corporeal machine, on the contrary, speak at pleasure; you have before you all your documents for ratiocination and decision; but, life once over,—when you have placed the limbs, closed the eyes, arranged the form,— can you arrange the mind?—the soul?'

'Excite no doubts in me, Harleigh!—my creed is fixed.'

'When sleep overtakes us,' he continued, 'and all, to the beholder, looks the picture of death, save that the breath still heaves the bosom;—what is it that guards entire, uninjured, the mind? the faculties? It is not our consciousness, —we have none! Where is the soul in that period? Gone it is not, for we are sensible to all that had preceded its suspension, the moment that we awake. Yet, in that state of periodical insensibility, what, but experience, could make those who view us believe that we could ever rise, speak, move, or think again? How inert is the body! How helpless, how useless, how incapable? Do we see who is near us? Do we hear who addresses us? Do we know when the most frightful crimes are committed by our sides? What, I demand, is our consciousness? We have not the most distant of any thing that passes around us: yet we open our eyes—and all is known, all is familiar again. We hear, we see, we feel, we understand!'

'Yes; but in that sleep, Harleigh, that mere mechanical repose of the animal, we still breathe; we are capable, therefore, of being restored to all our sensibilities, by a single touch, by a single start; 'tis but a separation that parts us from ourselves, as absence parts us from our friends. We yet live,—we yet, therefore, may meet again.'

'And why, when we live no longer, may we not also, Elinor, meet again?'

'Why?—Do you ask why?—Look round the old church-yards! See you not there the dispersion of our poor mouldered beings? Is not every bone the prey, —or the disgust,—of every animal? How, when scattered, commixed, broken, battered, how shall they ever again be collected, united, arranged, covered and coloured so as to appear regenerated?'

'But what, Elinor, is the fragility, or the dispersion of the body, to the solidity and the durability of the soul? Why are we to decide, that to see ourselves again, and again to view each other, such as we seem here, substance, or what we understand by it, is essential to our re-union hereafter? Do we not meet, act, talk, move, think with one another in our dreams? What is it which, then, embodies our ideas? which gives to our sight, in perfect form and likeness, those with whom we converse? which makes us conceive that we move, act, speak, and look, ourselves, with the same gesture, mien, and voice as when awake?'

'Dreams? pho!—they are but the nocturnal vagaries of the imagination.'

'And what, Elinor, is imagination? You will not call it a part of your body?'

'No; but the blood which still circulates in our veins, Harleigh, gives imagination its power.'

'But does the blood circulate in the veins of our parents, of our friends? of our

69

acquaintances? and of strangers whom we equally meet? yet we see them all; we converse with them all; we utter opinions; we listen to their answers. And how ably we sometimes argue! how characteristically those with whom we dispute reply! yet we do not imagine we guide them. We wait their opinions and decisions, in the same uncertainty and suspense, that we await them in our waking intercourse. We have the same fears of ill fortune; the same horrour of ill usage; the same ardour for success; the same feelings of sorrow, of joy, of hope, or of remorse, that animate or that torture us, in our daily occurrences. What new countries we visit! what strange sights we see! what delight, what anguish, what alarms, what pleasures, and what pains we experience! Yet in all this variety of incident, conversation, motion, feeling,— we seem, to those who look at us, but unintelligent and senseless, though still breathing clay.'

'Ay; but after all those scenes, we awake, Albert, we awake! But when do we awake from death? Death, the same experience tells us, is sleep eternal!'

'But in that sleep, also, are there no dreams? Are you sure of that? If, in our common sleep, there still subsists an active principle, that feels, speaks, invents, and only by awaking finds that the mind alone, and not the body has been working;—how are you so sure that no such active principle subsists in that sleep which you call eternal? Who has told you what passes where experience is at an end? Who has talked to you of "that bourne whence no traveller returns?" With the cessation, indeed, of warmth; with the stillness of those pulses which beat from circulating blood, all seems to end; but seems it not also to end when we fall into apoplexies? when we faint away? when we appear to be drowned? or when, by any means, life is casually suspended? Yet when those arts, that skill, of which even the success teaches not the principle, even the process discovers not the secret resources, draw back, by means intelligible and visible, but through causes indefinable, the fleeting breath to its corporeal habitation; animation instantly returns, and the soul, with all its powers, revives!'

'Ay, there, there, Albert, is the very point! If the soul were distinct from the body, why should not those who are recovered from drowning, suffocation, or other apparent death, be able to give some account of what passed in those periods when they seemed to be no more? And who has done it? No one, Harleigh! not a single renovated being, has explained away the doubts to which those suspensions of animation give rise.'

'And has any one explained, Elinor, why, though sometimes we have such wonders to relate of the scenes in which we have borne a part in our dreams, —we open our eyes, at other times, with no consciousness whatever, that we have, any way existed from the moment of closing them? The wants of refreshment and recruit of our corporeal machine, we all feel, and know; those of that part which is intellectual,—who is able to calculate? What, except the powers, can be more distinct than the exercises of the mind and of the body? Yet, though we see not the workings of what is intellectual; though they are known only by their effects,—does the student by the midnight oil require less rest from his mental fatigues,—whether he take it or not,—than the ploughman from his corporal labour? Is he not as wearied, as exhausted, after a day consigned to serious and unremitting study and reflection, as the labourer who has spent it in digging, paving, hewing, and sawing? Yet his body has been perfectly at peace; has not moved, has not made the smallest exertion.'

'And why, Harleigh? What is that, but because—'

'Hasten not, Elinor, thence, to your favourite conclusion, that soul and body, if wearied or rested together, are, therefore, one and the same thing: observation, and reflection, turned to other points of view, will shew you fresh reasons, and objects, every day, to disprove that identity: shew you, on one side, corporal force for supporting the bitterest grief of heart, with uninjured health; and, mental force, on the other side, for bearing the acutest bodily disorders with unimpaired intellectual vigour. How often do the most fragile machines, enwrap the stoutest minds? how often do the halest frames, encircle the feeblest intellects? All proves that the connexion between mind and body, however intimate, is not blended;—though where its limits begin, or where they end,—who can tell? But, who, also I repeat, can explain the phenomenon, by which, in the dead of the night, when we are completely insulated, and left in utter darkness, we firmly believe, nay, feel ourselves shone upon by the broad beams of day; and surrounded by society, with which we act, think, and reciprocate ideas?'

'Dreams, I must own, Albert, are strangely incomprehensible. How bodies can seem to appear, and voices to be heard, where all around is empty space, it is not easy to conceive!'

'Let this insolvable, and acknowledged difficulty, then, Elinor, in a circumstance which, though daily recurring, remains inexplicable, check any hardy decision of the cause why, after certain suspensions, the soul may resume its functions to our evident knowledge; yet why we can neither ascertain its departure, its continuance, nor its return, after others. Oh Elinor! mock not, but revere the impenetrable mystery of eternity! Ignorance is here our lot; presumption is our most useless infirmity. The mind and body after death must either be separate, or together. If together, as you assert, there is no proof attainable, that the soul partakes not of all the changes, all the dispersions, all the sufferings, and all the poor enjoyments, of what to us seems the lifeless, but which, in that case, is only the speechless carcase: if separate, as I believe,—whither goest thou, Oh soul! to what regions of bliss? —or what abysses of woe?'

'Harleigh, you electrify me! you convulse the whole train of my principles, my systems, my long cherished conviction!'

'Say, rather, Elinor, of your faith!—your faith in infidelity! Oh Elinor! why call you not, rather, upon faith to aid your belief? Faith, and revealed religion! The limited state of our positive perceptions, grants us no means for comparison, for judgment, or even for thought, but by analogy: ask yourself, then, Elinor,—What is there, even in immortality, more difficult of comprehension, than that indescribable daily occurrence, which all mankind equally, though unreflecting experience, of a total suspension of every species of living knowledge, of every faculty, of every sense,—called sleep? A suspension as big with matter for speculation and wonder, though its cessation is visible to us, as that last sleep, of which we view not the period.'

'Albert!—should you shake my creed,—shall I be better contented? or but yet more wretched?'

'Can Elinor think,—yet ask such a question? Can a prospect of a future state fail to offer a possibility of future happiness? Why wilfully reject a consolation that you have no means to disprove? What know you of this soul which you settle to be so easily annihilated? By what criterion do you judge it? You have none! save a general consciousness, that a something there is within us that mocks all search, yet that always is uppermost; that anticipates good or evil; that outruns all events; that feels the blow ere the flesh is touched; that expects the sound before the ear receives it; that, unseen, untraced, unknown, pervades, rules, animates all! that harbours thoughts, feelings, designs which no human force can controul; which no mortal, unaided by our own will, can discover; and which no aid whatever, either of our own or of others, can bring forward to any possible manifestation!'

'Alas, Harleigh! You shew me nonentity itself to be as doubtful as immortality! Of what wretched stuff are we composed! Which way must I now turn,—

'Lost and bewildered in my fruitless search,'[13]—

which way must I turn to develop truth? to comprehend my own existence! Oh Albert!—you almost make me wish to rest my perturbed mind where fools alone, I thought, found rest, or hypocrites have seemed to find it,—on Religion!'

'The feeling mind, dear Elinor, has no other serious serenity; no other hold from the black, cheerless, petrifying expectation of nullity. If, then, even a wish of light break through your dark despondence, read, study the Evangelists!—and truth will blaze upon you, with the means to find consolation.'

'Albert, I know now where I am!—You open to me possibilities that overwhelm me! My head seems bursting with fulness of struggling ideas!'

'Give them, Elinor, fair play, and they will soon, in return, give you tranquillity. Reflect only,—that that quality, that faculty, be its nature, its durability, and its purpose what they may, which the world at large agrees to call soul, has its universal comprehension from a something that is felt; not that is proved! Yet who, and where is the Atheist, the Deist, the Infidel of any description, gifted with the means to demonstrate, that, in quitting the body with the parting breath, it is necessarily extinct? that it may not, on the contrary, still BE, when speech and motion are no more? when our flesh is mingled with the dust, and our bones are dispersed by the winds? and BE, as while we yet exist, no part of our body, no single of our senses; never, while we seem to live, visible, yet never, when we seem to die, perishable? May it not, when, with its last sigh, it leaves the body, mingle with that vast expanse of air, which no instrument can completely analyse, and which our imperfect sight views but as empty space? May it not mount to upper regions, and enjoy purified bliss? May not all air be peopled with our departed friends, hovering around us, as sensible as we are unconscious? May not the uncumbered soul watch over those it loves? find again those it had lost? be received in the Heaven of Heavens, where it is destined,—not, Oh wretched idea!—to eternal sleep, inertness, annihilating dust;—but to life, to joy, to sweetest reminiscence, to tenderest re-unions, to grateful adoration to intelligence never ending! Oh! Elinor! keep for ever in mind, that if no mortal is gifted to prove that this is true,—neither is any one empowered to prove that it is false!'

'Oh delicious idea!' cried Elinor, rising: 'Oh image of perfection! Oh Albert! conquering Albert! I hope,—I hope;—my soul may be immortal!—Pray for me, Albert! Pray that I may dare offer up prayers for myself!—Send me your Christian divine to guide me on my way; and may your own heaven bless you, peerless Albert! for ever!—Adieu! adieu! adieu!'—

Fervently, then, clasping her hands, she sunk, with overpowering feelings, upon her knees.

Juliet came forward to support her; and Harleigh, deeply gratified, though full of commiseration, eagerly undertook the commission; and, echoing back her blessing, without daring to utter a word to Juliet, slowly quitted the spot.

CHAPTER LXXXVI

Elinor, for a considerable time, remained in the same posture, ruminating, in silent abstraction; yet giving, from time to time, emphatic, though involuntary utterance, to short and incoherent sentences. 'A spirit immortal!—' 'Resurrection of the Dead!—' 'A life to come!—' 'Oh Albert! is there, then, a region where I may hope to see thee again!'

Suddenly, at length, seeming to recollect herself, 'Pardon,' she cried, 'Albert, my strangeness,—queerness,—oddity,—what will you call it? I am not the less,—O no! O no! penetrated by your impressive reasoning—Albert!—'

She lifted up her head, and, looking around, exclaimed, with an air of consternation, 'Is he gone?'

She arose, and with more firmness, said, 'He is right! I meant not,—and I ought not to see him any more;—though dearer to my eyes is his sight, than life or light!—'

Looking, then, earnestly forwards, as if seeking him, 'Farewell, Oh Albert!' she cried: 'We now, indeed, are parted for ever! To see thee again, would sink me into the lowest abyss of contempt,—and I would far rather bear thy hatred!—Yet hatred?—from that soul of humanity!—what violence must be put upon its nature! And how cruel to reverse such ineffable philanthropy!— No!—hate me not, my Albert!—It shall be my own care that thou shalt not despise me!'

Slowly she then walked away, followed silently by Juliet, who durst not address her. Anxiously she looked around, till, at some distance, she descried a horseman. It was Harleigh. She stopped, deeply moved, and seemed inwardly to bless him. But, when he was no longer in sight, she no longer restrained her anguish, and, casting herself upon the turf, groaned rather than wept, exclaiming, 'Must I live—yet behold thee no more!—Will neither sorrow, nor despair, nor even madness kill me?—Must nature, in her decrepitude, alone bring death to Elinor?'

Rising, then, and vainly trying again to descry the horse, 'All, all is gone!' she cried, 'and I dare not even die!—All, all is gone, from the lost, unhappy Elinor, but life and misery!'

Turning, then, with quickness to Juliet, while pride and shame dried her eyes, 'Ellis,' she said, 'let him not know I murmur!—Let not his last hearing of Elinor be disgrace! Tell him, on the contrary, that his friendship shall not be thrown away; nor his arguments be forgotten, or unavailing: no! I will weigh every opinion, every sentiment that has fallen from him, as if every word, unpolluted by human ignorance or informity, had dropt straight from heaven! I will meditate upon religion: I will humble myself to court resignation. I will fly hence, to avoid all temptation of ever seeing him more!—and to distract my wretchedness by new scenes. Oh Albert!—I will earn thy esteem by acquiescence in my lot, that here,—even here,—I may taste the paradise of alluring thee to include me in thy view of happiness hereafter!'

Her foreign servant, then, came in view, and she made a motion to him with her hand for her carriage. She awaited it in profound mental absorption, and, when it arrived, placed herself in it without speaking.

Juliet, full of tender pity, could no longer forbear saying, 'Adieu, Madam! and may peace re-visit your generous heart!'

Elinor, surprized and softened, looked at her with an expression of involuntary admiration, as she answered, 'I believe you to be good, Ellis!—I exonerate you from all delusory arts; and, internally, I never thought you guilty,—or I had never feared you! Fool! mad fool, that I have been, I am my own executioner! my distracting impatience to learn the depth of my danger, was what put you together! taught you to know, to appreciate one another! With my own precipitate hand, I have dug the gulph into which I am fallen! Your dignified patience, your noble modesty—Oh fatal Ellis!—presented a contrast that plunged a dagger into all my efforts! Rash, eager ideot! I conceived suspense to be my greatest bane!—Oh fool! eternal fool!—self-willed, and self-destroying!—for the single thrill of one poor moment's returning doubt—I would not suffer martyrdom!'

She wept, and hid her face within the carriage; but, holding out her hand to Juliet, 'Adieu, Ellis!' she cried, 'I struggle hardly not to wish you any ill; and I have never given you my malediction: yet Oh!—that you had never been born!'—

She snatched away her hand, and precipitately drew up all the blinds, to hide her emotion; but, presently, letting one of them down, called out, with resumed vivacity, and an air of gay defiance, 'Marry him, Ellis!—marry him at once! I have always felt that I should be less mad, if my honour called upon me for reason!—my honour and my pride!'

The groom demanded orders.

'Drive to the end of the world!' she answered, impatiently, 'so you ask me no questions!' and, forcibly adding, 'Farewell, too happy Ellis!' she again drew up all the blinds, and, in a minute, was out of sight.

Juliet deplored her fate with the sincerest concern; and ruminated upon her virtues, and attractive qualities, till their drawbacks diminished from her view, and left nothing but unaffected wonder, that Harleigh could resist them: 'twas a wonder, nevertheless, that every feeling of her heart, in defiance of every conflict, rose, imperiously, to separate from regret.

At the cottage, she found her recovered property, which she now concluded, —for her recollection was gone,—that she had dropt upon her entrance into the room occupied by Harleigh, before she had perceived that it was not empty.

Here, too, almost immediately afterwards, her messenger returned with a letter, which had remained more than a week at the post-office; whither it had been sent back by the farmer, who had refused to risk advancing the postage.

The letter was from Gabriella, and sad, but full of business. She had just received a hurrying summons from Mr de ——, her husband, to join him at Teignmouth, in Devonshire; and, for family-reasons, which ought not to be resisted, to accompany him abroad. Mr de —— had been brought by an accidental conveyance to Torbay; whence, through a peculiarly favourable opportunity, he was to sail to his place of destination. He charged her to use the utmost expedition; and, to spare the expence of a double journey, and the difficulties of a double passport, for and from London, he should procure permission to meet her at Teignmouth; where they might remain till their vessel should be ready; the town of Brixham, within Torbay, being filled with sailors, and unfit for female residence.

Gabriella owned, that she had nothing substantial, nor even rational, to oppose to this plan; though her heart would be left in the grave, the English grave of her adored child. She had relinquished, therefore, her shop, and paid the rent, and her debts; and obtained money for the journey by the sale of all her commodities. She then tenderly entreated, if no insurmountable obstacles forbid it, that Juliet would be of their party; and gave the direction of Mr de —— at Teignmouth.

Not a moment could Juliet hesitate upon joining her friend; though whether or not she should accompany her abroad, she left for decision at their meeting. She greatly feared the delay in receiving the letter might make her arrive too late; but the experiment was well worth trial; and she reached the beautifully situated small town of Teignmouth the next morning.

She drove to the lodging of which Gabriella had given the direction; where she had the affliction to learn, that the lady whom she described, and her husband, had quitted Teignmouth the preceding evening for Torbay.

She instantly demanded fresh horses, for following them; but the postilion said, that he must return directly to Exeter, with his chaise; and enquired where she would alight. Where she might most speedily, she answered, find means to proceed.

The postilion drove her, then, to a large lodging-house; but the town was so full of company, as it was the season for bathing, that there was no chaise immediately ready; and she was obliged to take possession of a room, till some horses returned.

As soon as she had deposited her baggage, she resolved upon walking back to the late lodging of Gabriella, to seek some further information.

In re-passing a gallery, which led from her chamber to the stairs, she perceived, upon a band-box, left at the half-closed door of what appeared to be the capital apartment, the loved name of Lady Aurora Granville.

Joy, hope, fondness, and every pleasurable emotion, danced suddenly in her breast; and, chacing away, by surprize, all fearful caution, irresistibly impelled her to push open the door.

All possibility of concealment was, she knew, now at an end; and, with it, finished her long forbearance. How sweet to cast herself, at length, under so benign a protection! to build upon the unalterable sweetness of Lady Aurora for a consolatory reception, and openly to claim her support!

Filled with these delighting ideas, she gently entered the room. It was empty; but, the door to an inner apartment being open, she heard the soft voice of Lady Aurora giving directions to some servant.

While she hesitated whether, at once, to venture on, or to send in some message, a chambermaid, coming out with another band-box, shut the inner door.

The dress of Juliet was no longer such as to make her appearance in a capital apartment suspicious; and the chambermaid civily enquired whom she was pleased to want.

'Lady Aurora Granville,' she hesitatingly answered; adding that she would tap at her ladyship's door herself, and begging that the maid would not wait.

The maid, busy and active, hurried off. Quickly, then, though softly, Juliet stept forward; but at the door, trembling and full of fears, she stopt short; and the sight of pen, ink, and paper upon a table, determined her to commit her attempt to writing.

Seizing a sheet of paper, without sitting down, and in a hand scarcely legible, she began,

'Is Lady Aurora Granville still the same Lady Aurora, the kind, the benignant, the indulgent Lady Aurora,—' when the sound of another voice, a voice more discordant, if possible, than that of Lady Aurora had been melodious, reached her ear from under the window: it was that of Mrs Howel.

As shaking now with terrour as before she had been trembling with hope, she rolled up her paper; and was hurrying it into her work-bag, which had been returned to her by Harleigh; when the chambermaid, re-entering the room, stared at her with some surprize, demanding whether she had seen her ladyship.

'No; ... I believe ... she is occupied,' Juliet, stammering, answered; and flew along the gallery back to her chamber.

That Lady Aurora should be under the care of Mrs Howel, who was the nearest female relation of Lord Denmeath, could give no surprize to Juliet; but the impulse which had urged her forward, had only painted to her a precious interview with Lady Aurora alone; for how venture to reveal herself in presence of so hard, so inimical a witness? The very idea, joined to the terrible apprehension of irritating Lord Denmeath, to aid some new attack from her legal persecutor; so damped her rising joy, so repressed her buoyant hopes, that, to avoid the insupportable repetition of injurious interrogatories, painful explanations, and insulting incredulity, she decided, if she could join Gabriella at Torbay, to accompany her to her purposed retreat; and there to await either intelligence of the Bishop, or an open summons from her own family.

She hastened, therefore, to the late lodging of Gabriella; where, upon a more minute investigation, she found, that a message had been left, in case a lady should call to enquire for Madame de ——, to say, that the small vessel in which M. de —— and herself were humanely to be received as passengers, was ready to sail; and to promise to write upon their landing; and to endeavour to fix upon some means of re-union. The lady, the lodging-people said, had lost all hope of her friend's arrival, but had left that message in case of accidents.

More eagerly than ever, Juliet now enquired for any kind of carriage; but the town was full, and every vehicle was engaged till the next morning.

The next morning opened with a new and cruel disappointment: the chambermaid came with excuses, that no chaise could be had, till towards evening, as the Honourable Mrs Howel had engaged all the horses, to carry herself and her people to Chudleigh-park.

Dreadful to the impatience of Juliet was such a loss of time; yet she shrunk from all appeal, upon her prior rights, with Mrs Howel.

Still, not to render impossible, before her departure, an interview, after which her heart was sighing, with Lady Aurora, she addressed to her a few lines.

'To the Right Honourable
Lady Aurora Granville.

'Brought hither in search of the friend of my earlier youth, what have been my perturbation, my hope, my fear, at the sound of the voice of her whom, proudly and fondly, it is my first wish to be permitted to love, and to claim as the friend of my future days! Ah, Lady Aurora! my inmost soul is touched and moved!—nevertheless, not to press upon the difficulties of your delicacy, nor to take advantage of the softness of your sensibility, I go hence without imploring your support or countenance. I quit again this loved land, scarcely known, though devoutly revered, to watch and wait,—far, far off!—for tidings of my future lot: I go to join the generous guardian of my orphan life,—till I know whether I may hope to be acknowledged by a brother! I go to dwell with my noble adopted sister,—till I learn whether I may be recalled, to be owned by one still nearer,—and who alone can be still dearer!'

She gave this paper sealed, for delivery, to the chambermaid; saying that she was going to take a long walk; and desiring, should there be any answer, that it might carefully be kept for her return.

This measure was to give Lady Aurora time to reflect, whether or not she should demand an explanation of the note; rather than to surprize the first eager impulse of her kindness.

She then bent her steps towards the sea-side; but, though it was still very early, there was so much company upon the sands, taking exercise before, or after bathing, that she soon turned another way; and, invited by the verdant freshness of the prospects, rambled on for a considerable time: at first, with no other design than to while away a few hours; but, afterwards, to give to those hours the pleasure ever new, ever instructive, of viewing and studying the works of nature; which, on this charming spot, now awfully noble, now elegantly simple; where the sea and the land, the one sublime in its sameness, the other, exhilarating in its variety, seem to be presented, as if in primeval lustre, to the admiring eye of a meditative being.

She clambered up various rocks, nearly to their summit, to enjoy, in one grand perspective, the stupendous expansion of the ocean, glittering with the brilliant rays of a bright and cloudless sky: dazzled, she descended to their base, to repose her sight upon the soft, yet lively tint of the green turf, and the rich, yet mild hue of the downy moss. Almost sinking, now, from the scorching beams of a nearly vertical sun, she looked round for some umbrageous retreat; but, refreshed the next moment, by salubrious sea-breezes, by the coolness of the rocks, or by the shade of the trees, she remained stationary, and charmed; a devoutly adoring spectatress of the lovely, yet magnificent scenery encircling her; so vast in its glory, so impressive in its details, of wild, varied nature, apparently in its original state.

When at length, she judged it to be right to return, upon coming within sight of the lodging-house, she saw a carriage at the door, into which some lady was mounting.

Could it be Lady Aurora?—could she so depart, after reading her letter? She retreated till the carriage drove off; and then, at the foot of the stairs, met the chambermaid; of whom she eagerly asked, whether there were any letter, or message, for her, from Lady Aurora.

The maid answered No; her ladyship was gone away without saying any thing.

The words 'gone away' extremely affected Juliet, who, in ascending to her room, wept bitterly at such a desertion; even while concluding it to have been exacted by Mrs Howel.

She rang the bell, to enquire whether she might now have a chaise.

The chambermaid told her that she must come that very moment to speak to a lady.

'What lady?' cried Juliet, ever awake to hope; 'Is Lady Aurora Granville come back?'

No, no; Lady Aurora was gone to Chudleigh.

'What lady then?'

Mrs Howel, the maid answered, who ordered her to come that instant.

''Tis a mistake,' said Juliet, with spirit; 'you must seek some other person to whom to deliver such a message!'

The maid would have asserted her exactitude in executing her commission; but Juliet, declining to hear her, insisted upon being left.

Extremely disturbed, she could suggest no reason why Mrs Howel should remain, when Lady Aurora was gone; nor divine whether her letter were voluntarily unanswered; or whether it had even been delivered; nor what might still instigate the unrestrained arrogance of Mrs Howel.

In a few minutes, the chambermaid returned, to acquaint her, that, if she did not come immediately, Mrs Howel would send for her in another manner.

Too indignant, now, for fear, Juliet, said that she had no answer to give to such a message; and charged the maid not to bring her any other.

Another, nevertheless, and ere she had a moment to breathe, followed; which was still more peremptory, and to which the chambermaid sneeringly added,

'You wonna let me look into youore work-bag, wull y?'

'Why should you look into my work-bag?'

'Nay, it ben't I as do want it; it be Maddam Howel.'

'And for what purpose?'

'Nay, I can't zay; but a do zay a ha' lost a bank-note.'

'And what have I, or my work-bag, to do with that?'

'Nay I don't know; but it ben't I ha' ta'en it. And it ben't I—'

She stopt, grinning significantly; but, finding that Juliet deigned not to ask an explanation, went on: 'It ben't I as husselled zomat into my work-bag, in zuch a peck o' troubles, vor to hide it; it ben't I, vor there be no mortal mon, nor womon neither, I be afeared of; vor I do teake no mon's goods but my own.'

Juliet now was thunderstruck. If a bank-note were missing, appearances, from her silently entering and quitting the room, were certainly against her; and though it could not be difficult to clear away such a suspicion, it was shocking, past endurance, to have such a suspicion to clear.

While she hesitated what to reply, the maid, not doubting but that her embarrassment was guilt, triumphantly continued her own defence; saying, whoever might be suspected, it could not be she, for she did not go into other people's rooms, not she! to peer about, and see what was to be seen; nor say she was going to call upon grand gentlefolks, when she was not going to do any such thing; not she! nor tear paper upon other people's tables, to roll things up, and poke them into her work-bag; not she! she had nothing to hide, for there was nothing she took, so there was nothing she had to be ashamed of, not she!

She then mutteringly walked off; but almost instantly returned, desiring to know, in the name of Mrs Howel, whether Miss Ellis preferred that the business of her examination should be terminated, before proper witnesses, in her own room.

Juliet, thus assailed, urged by judgment, and a sense of propriety, struggled against personal feelings and fears; and resolved to rescue not only herself, but her family, from the disgrace of a public interrogatory. She walked, therefore, straight forward to the apartment of Mrs Howel; determined to own, without delay, her birth and situation, rather than submit to any indignity.

At the entrance, she made way for the chambermaid to announce her; but when she heard that voice, which, to her shocked ears, sounded far more hoarse, more harsh, and more coarse than the raven's croak, her spirits nearly forsook her. To cast herself thus upon the powerful enmity of Lord Denmeath, with no kind Lady Aurora at hand, to soften the hazardous tale, by her benignant pity; no generous Lord Melbury within call, to resist perverse incredulity, by spontaneous support, and promised protection:—'twas dreadful!—Yet no choice now remained, no possible resource; she must meet her fate, or run away as a culprit.

The latter she utterly disdained; and, at the words, loudly spoken, from the inner room, 'Order her to appear!' she summoned to her aid all that she possessed of pride or of dignity, to disguise her apprehensions; and obeyed the imperious mandate.

Mrs Howel, seated upon an easy chair, received her with an air of prepared scorn; in which, nevertheless, was mixed some surprize at the elegance, yet propriety, of her attire. 'Young woman,' she sternly said, 'what part is this you are acting? And what is it you suppose will be its result? Can you imagine that you are to brave people of condition with impunity? You have again dared to address, clandestinely, and by letter, a young lady of quality, whom you know to be forbidden to afford you any countenance. You have entered my apartment under false pretences; you have been detected precipitately quitting it, thrusting something into your work-bag, evidently taken from my table.'—

Juliet now felt her speech restored by contempt. 'I by no means intended, Madam,' she drily answered, 'to have intruded upon your benevolence. The sheet of paper which I took was to write to Lady Aurora Granville; and I imagined,—mistakenly, it seems,—that it was already her ladyship's.'

The calmness of Juliet operated to produce a storm in Mrs Howel that fired all her features; though, deeming it unbecoming her rank in life, to shew anger to a person beneath her, she subdued her passion into sarcasm, and said, 'Her ladyship, then, it seems, is to provide the paper with which you write to her, as well as the clothes with which you wait upon her? That she refuses herself whatever is not indispensable, in order to make up a secret purse, has long been clear to me; and I now, in your assumed garments, behold the application of her privations!'

'Oh Lady Aurora! lovely and loved Lady Aurora! have you indeed this kindness for me! this heavenly goodness!'—interrupted, from a sensibility that she would not seek to repress, the penetrated Juliet.

'Unparalleled assurance!' exclaimed Mrs Howel. 'And do you think thus triumphantly to gain your sinister ends? no! Lady Aurora will never see your letter! I have already dispatched it to my Lord Denmeath.'

The spirit of Juliet now instantly sunk: she felt herself again betrayed into the power of her persecutor; again seized; and trembled so exceedingly, that she with difficulty kept upon her feet.

Mrs Howel exultingly perceived her advantage. 'What,' she haughtily demanded, 'has brought you hither? And why are you here? If, indeed, you approach the sea-side with a view to embark, and return whence you came, I am far from offering any impediment to so befitting a measure. My Lord Denmeath, I have reason to believe, would even assist it. Speak, young woman! have you sense enough of the unbecoming situation in which you now stand, to take so proper a course for getting to your home?'

'My home!' repeated Juliet, casting up her eyes, which, bedewed with tears at the word, she then covered with her handkerchief.

'If to go thither be your intention,' said Mrs Howel, 'the matter may be accommodated; speak, then.'

'The little, Madam, that I mean to say,' cried Juliet, 'I must beg leave to address to you when you are alone.' For the waiting-woman still remained at the side of the toilette-table.

'At length, then,' said Mrs Howel, much gratified, though always scornful; 'you mean to confess?' And she told her woman to hasten the packing up, and then to step into the next room.

'Think, however;' she continued; 'deliberate, in this interval, upon what you are going to do. I have already heard the tale which I have seen, by your letter, you hint at propagating; heard it from my Lord Denmeath himself. But so idle a fabrication, without a single proof, or document, in its support, will only be considered as despicable. If that, therefore, is the subject upon which you purpose to entertain me in this *tête à tête*, be advised to change it, untried. Such stale tricks are only to be played upon the inexperienced. You may well blush, young woman! I am willing to hope it is with shame.'

'You force me, Madam, to speak!' indignantly cried Juliet; 'though you will not, thus publicly, force me to an explanation. For your own sake, Madam, for decency's, if not for humanity's sake, press me no further, till we are alone! or the blush with which you upbraid me, now, may hereafter be yours! And not a blush like mine, from the indignation of innocence injured—yet unsullied; but the blush of confusion and shame; latent, yet irrepressible!'

Rage, now, is a word inadequate to express the violent feelings of Mrs Howel, which, nevertheless, she still strove to curb under an appearance of disdain. 'You would spare me, then,' she cried, 'this humiliation? And you suppose I can listen to such arrogance? Undeceive yourself, young woman; and produce the contents of your work-bag at once, or expect its immediate seizure for examination, by an officer of justice.'

'What, Madam, do you mean?' cried Juliet, endeavouring, but not very successfully, to speak with unconcern.

'To allow you the choice of more, or fewer witnesses to your boasted innocence!'

'If your curiosity, Madam,' said Juliet, more calmly, yet not daring any longer to resist, 'is excited to take an inventory of my small property, I must endeavour to indulge it.'

She was preparing to untie the strings of her work-bag; when a sudden recollection of the bank-notes of Harleigh, for the possession of which she could give no possible account, checked her hand, and changed her countenance.

Mrs Howel, perceiving her embarrassment, yet more haughtily said, 'Will you deliver your work-bag, young woman, to Rawlins?'

'No, Madam!' answered Juliet, reviving with conscious dignity; 'I will neither so far offend myself at this moment,—nor you for every moment that shall follow! I can deliver it only into your own hands.'

'Enough!' cried Mrs Howel. 'Rawlins, order Hilson to enquire out the magistrate of this village, and to desire that he will send to me some peace-officer immediately.'

She then opened the door of a small inner room, into which she shut herself, with an air of deadly vengeance.

Mrs Rawlins, at the same time, passed to the outer room, to summon Hilson.

Juliet, confounded, remained alone. She looked from one side to the other; expecting either that Mrs Howel would call upon her, or that Mrs Rawlins would return for further orders. Neither of them re-appeared, or spoke.

Alarmed, now, yet more powerfully than disgusted, she compelled herself to tap at the door of Mrs Howel, and to beg admission.

She received no answer. A second and a third attempt failed equally. Affrighted more seriously, she hastened to the outer room; where a man, Hilson, she supposed, was just quitting Mrs Rawlins.

'Mrs Rawlins,' she cried; 'I beseech you not to send any one off, till you have received fresh directions.'

Mrs Rawlins desired to know whether this were the command of her lady.

'It will be,' Juliet replied, 'when I have spoken to her again.'

Mrs Rawlins answered, that her lady was always accustomed to be obeyed at once; and told Hilson to make haste.

Juliet entreated for only a moment's delay; but the man would not listen.

Though from justice Juliet could have nothing to fear, the idea of being forced to own herself, when a peace-officer was sent for, to avoid being examined as a criminal, filled her with such horrour and affright, that, calling out, 'Stop! stop! I beseech you stop!—' she ran after the man, with a precipitate eagerness, that made her nearly rush into the arms of a gentleman, who, at that moment, having just passed by Hilson, filled up the way.

Without looking at him, she sought to hurry on; but, upon his saying, 'I ask pardon, Ma'am, for barricading your passage in this sort;' she recognized the voice of her first patron, the Admiral.

Charmed with the hope of succour, 'Is it you, Sir?' she cried. 'Oh Sir, stop that person!—Call to him! Bid him return! I implore you!—'

'To be sure I will, ma'am!' answered he, courteously taking off his hat, though appearing much amazed; and hallooing after Hilson, 'Hark'ee, my lad! be so kind to veer about a bit.'

Hilson, not venturing to shew disrespect to the uniform of the Admiral, stood still.

The Admiral then, putting on his hat, and conceiving his business to be done, was passing on; and Hilson grinning at the short-lived impediment, was continuing his route; but the calls and pleadings of Juliet made the Admiral turn back, and, in a tone of authority, and with the voice of a speaking trumpet, angrily cry, 'Halloo, there! Tack about and come hither, my lad! What do you go t'other way for, when a lady calls you? By George, if they had you aboard, they'd soon teach you better manners!'

Juliet, again addressing him, said, 'Oh Sir! how good you are! how truly benevolent!—Detain him but till I speak with his lady, and I shall be obliged to you eternally!'

'To be sure I will, Ma'am!' answered the wondering Admiral. 'He sha'n't pass me. You may depend upon that.'

Juliet, meaning now to make her sad and forced confession, re-entered the first apartment; and was soliciting, through Mrs Rawlins, for an audience with Mrs Howel; when Hilson, surlily returning, preceded the petitioner to his lady; and complained that he had been set upon by a bully of the young woman's.

Mrs Howel, coming forth, with a wrath that was deaf to prayer or representation, gave orders that the master of the house should be called to account for such an insult to one of her people.

The master of the house appearing, made a thousand excuses for what had happened; but said that he could not be answerable for people's falling to words upon the stairs.

Mrs Howel insisted upon reparation; and that those who had affronted her people should be told to go out of the house; or she herself would never enter it again.

The landlord declared that he did not know how to do such a thing, for the gentleman was his honour the Admiral; who was come to spend two or three days there, from the shipping at Torbay.

If it were a general-officer who had acted thus, she said, he could certainly give some reason for his conduct; and she desired the landlord to ask it of him in her name.

In vain, during this debate, Juliet made every concession, save that of delivering her work-bag to the scrutiny of Mrs Rawlins; nothing less would satisfy the enraged Mrs Howel, who resisted all overtures for a *tête à tête*; determined publicly to humble the object of her wrath.

The Admiral, who was found standing sentinel at the door, desired an audience of the lady himself.

Mrs Howel accorded it with readiness; ordering Hilson, Mrs Rawlins, and the landlord, to remain in the room.

CHAPTER LXXXVII

Mrs Howel received the Admiral, seated, with an air of state, upon her arm-chair; at one side of which stood Mrs Rawlins, and at the other Hilson. The landlord was stationed near the door; and Juliet, indignant, though trembling, placed herself at a window; determining rather, with whatever mortification, to seek the protection of the Admiral, than to avow who she was thus publicly, thus disgracefully, and thus compulsorily.

The Admiral entered with the martial air of a man used to command; and whose mind was made up not to be put out of his way. He bestowed, nevertheless, three low bows, with great formality, to the sex of Mrs Howel; to the first of which she arose and courtsied, returning the two others by an inclination of the head, and bidding Hilson bring the Admiral a chair.

The Admiral, having adjusted himself, his hat, and his sword to his liking, said, 'I wish you good morning, Ma'am. You won't take it amiss, I hope, that I make free to wait upon you myself, for the sake of having a small matter of discourse with you, about a certain chap that I understand to be one of your domestics; a place whereof, if I may judge by what I have seen of him, he is not over and above worthy.'

'If any of my people, Sir,' answered Mrs Howel, 'have forgotten what is due to an officer of your rank, I shall take care to make them sensible of my displeasure.'

The Admiral, much gratified, made her a low bow, saying, 'A lady, Ma'am, such as I suppose you to be, can't fail having a right way of thinking. But that sort of gentry, as I have taken frequent note, have an ugly kind of a knack, of treating people rather short that have got a favour to ask; the which I don't uphold. And this is the main reason that I think it right to give you an item of my opinion upon this matter, respecting that lad; who just now, in my proper view, let a young gentlewoman call and squall after him, till she was black in the face, without so much as once veering round, to say, Pray, Ma'am, what do you please to want?'

Hilson, now, triumphant that he could plead his haste to obey the commands of his lady, was beginning an affronted self-defence; when the Admiral, accidentally perceiving Juliet, hastily arose; and in a fit of unrestrained choler, clinching his double fist at Hilson, cried, 'Why what sort of a fellow are you, Sir? to bring me a chair while you see a lady standing? Which do you take to be strongest? An old weather beaten tar, such as I am; or a poor weak female, that could not lend a hand to the pump, thof the vessel were going to the bottom?'

Approaching Juliet, then with his own arm-chair, he begged her to be seated; saying, 'The lad will take care to bring another to me, I warrant him! A person who has got a scrap of gold-lace sewed upon his jacket, is seldom overlooked by that kind of gentry; for which reason I make no great account of complaisance, when I am dizened in my full dress uniform,—which, by the way, is a greater ceremony-monger than this, by thus much (measuring with his finger) more of tinsel!'

Juliet, gratefully thanking him, but declining his offer, thought this an opportunity not to be missed, to attempt, under his courageous auspice, to escape. She courtsied to him, therefore, and was walking away: but Mrs Howel, swelling with ire, already, at such civility to a creature whom she had condemned to scorn, now flamed with passion, and openly told the landlord, to let that young woman pass at his peril.

Juliet, who saw in the anger which was mixed with the amazement of the Admiral, that she had a decided defender at hand, collected her utmost presence of mind, and, advancing to Mrs Howel, said, 'I have offered to you, Madam, any explanation you may require alone; but in public I offer you none!'

'If you think yourself still dealing with a novice of the inexperience of sixteen,' answered Mrs Howel, 'you will find yourself mistaken. I will neither trust to the arts of a private recital, nor save your pride from a public examination.'

Then, addressing the Admiral, 'All yesterday morning, Sir,' she continued, 'I had sundry articles, such as rings, bank-notes, and letters of value, dispersed in my apartment, from a security that it was sacred; but the chambermaid informs me, that she caught this young woman entering it, under pretence of waiting upon a young lady, then in the inner room; and the same chambermaid, an hour after, found that she was still here; and endeavouring to conceal, in her work-bag something that she had wrapt into a sheet of paper, that was confessedly pilfered from my table.'—

The Admiral, observing, in the midst of the disturbance of Juliet at this attack, an air of offended dignity, which urged him to believe that she was innocent, unhesitatingly answered, ''Tis an old saying, Madam, and a wise one, that standers-by see the most of the game; and I have taken frequent note, that we are all of one mind, till we have heard two sides of the question: for which reason I hold it but fair, that the young gentlewoman should be asked what she has to say for herself.'

'Can you suppose, Sir,' said Mrs Howel, the veins of whose face and throat now looked bursting, 'that I mean to canvass this matter upon terms of equality? that I intend to be my own pleader against a pauper and an impostor?'—

Juliet here held her hand upon her forehead, as if scarcely able to sustain the indignant pain with which she was seized; and the fierce frown of the Admiral, showed his gauntlet not merely ready to be flung on the ground, but almost in the face of her adversary; Mrs Howel, however, went on.

'I do not pretend to affirm that any thing has been purloined; but the circumstances of the case are certainly extraordinary; and I should be sorry to run the risk of wrongfully suspecting,—should something hereafter be missing,—any of my own people. I demand, therefore, immediately, an explanation of this transaction.'

The Admiral, full of angry feelings as he looked at the panting Juliet, replied, himself; 'To my seeming, Madam, the short cut to the truth in this business, would be for you to cast an eye upon your own affairs; which I doubt not but you will find in very good trim; and if you should like to know what passes in my mind, I must needs make bold to remark, that I think the so doing would be more good natured, by a fellow-creature, than putting a young gentlewoman out of countenance by talking so high: which, moreover, proves no fact.'

'I am infinitely indebted to you, Sir, for the honour of your reprimand,' Mrs Howel, affectedly bowing, answered; 'which I should not have incurred, had it not appeared to me, that it would be far more troublesome to my people, to take an exact review of my various and numerous trinkets and affairs, than for an innocent person to display the contents of a small work-bag.'

'Nay, that is but reasonable,' said the Admiral; 'I won't say to the contrary. And I make small doubt, but that the young gentlewoman desires, in like manner with ourselves, that all should be fair and above board. The work-bag, I'll bet you all I am worth, has not a gimcrack in it that is not her own.'

Juliet, to whom the consciousness was ever uppermost of the suspicious bank-notes, felt by no means inclined to submit to an examination. Again, therefore, and with firmness, she declined giving any communication, but in a private interview with Mrs Howel.

Mrs Howel, now, had not a doubt remaining, that something had been stolen; and, still more desirous to disgrace the culprit, than to recover her property, she declared, that she was perfectly ready to add to the number of witnesses, but resolutely fixed not to diminish it; public shame being the best antidote that could be offered, against those arts by which youth and credulity had been duped.

Juliet now looked down; embarrassed, distressed, yet colouring with resentment. The Admiral, not conceiving her situation; nor being able to comprehend the difficulty of displaying the contents of a work-bag, approached her, and strove to give her courage.

'Come!' he cried, 'young gentlewoman! don't be faint-hearted. Let the lady have her way. I always like to have my own, which makes me speak up for others. Besides which, I have no great opinion of quarrelling for straws. We are none of us the nearer the mark for falling to loggerheads: for which reason I make it a rule never to lose my temper myself; except when I am provoked; so untie your work-bag, young gentlewoman. I'll engage that it will do you no discredit, by the very turn of your eye; for I don't know that, to my seeming, I ever saw a modester look of a face.'

This harangue was uttered in a tone of good-humoured benevolence, that seemed seeking to raise her spirits; yet with an expression of compassion, that indicated a tender feeling for her disturbance; while the marked integrity, and honest frankness of his own character, with a high sense of honour, and a sincere love of virtue, beamed benignly, as he looked at her, in every feature of his kind, though furrowed face.

Juliet was sensibly touched by his goodness and liberality, which surprized from her all precaution; and the concession which she had refused to arrogant menace, she spontaneously granted, to secure the good will of her ancient, though unconscious friend. Raising, therefore, her eyes, in which an expression of gratitude took place of that of sadness, 'I will not, Sir,' she said, 'resist your counsel; though I have in nothing forfeited my inherent right to the inviolability of my property.'

She then put her work-bag into his own hands.

He received it with a bow down to the ground; while joy almost capered in his old eyes; and, exultingly turning to Mrs Howel, 'To my seeming, Madam,' he said, 'this young gentlewoman is as well-behaved a girl, as a man might wish to meet with, from one side the globe to the t'other; and I respect her accordingly. And, if I were to do so unhandsome a thing, as to poke and peer into her baggage, after seeing her comport herself so genteelly, I won't deny but I should merit a cat-o'-nine tails, better than many an honest tar that receives them. And, therefore, I hope, now, Madam, you will give back to the young gentlewoman your good opinion, in like manner as I, here, give her back her work-bag.'

And then, with another profound bow, and a flourish of his hand, that shewed his pleasure in the part which he was taking, he was returning to Juliet her property; when he was startled by an ungovernable gust of wrath, from the utterly enraged Mrs Howel, who exclaimed, 'If you dare take it, young woman, unexamined, 'tis to a justice of the peace, and not to a sea-officer, that you will deliver it another time!'

Juliet, certain, whatever might be her ultimate fate, that her birth and family must, inevitably, be soon discovered, revolted from this menace; and determined, rather than submit to any further indignity, to risk casting herself, at once, upon the gentleman-like humanity of the Admiral. Unintimidated, therefore, by the alarming threat, which, heretofore, had appalled her, she steadily held out her hand, and received, from the old officer, in graceful silence, the proffered work-bag.

There is nothing which so effectually oversets an accusing adversary, as self-possession; self-possession, which, if unaffected, is the highest attribute of fearless innocence; if assumed, the most consummate address of skilful art. Called, therefore, from rage to shame, by the calmness of Juliet, Mrs Howel constrained herself to resume her air of solemn importance; and, perceiving the piqued look of the Admiral, at her slighting manner of naming sea-officers, she courteously said, 'Permit me, Sir, as you are so good as to enter into this affair, to state to you that this young woman comes from abroad; and has no ostensible method of living in this country: will it not, then, be more consonant to prudence and decorum, that she should hasten to return whence she came?'

'Madam,' answered the Admiral, coldly, 'I never give advice upon the onset of a question; that is to say, never till I see that one thing had better be done than another. I have no great taste for groping in the dark; wherefore, when I don't rightly make out what a person would be at, I think the best mode to keep clear of a dispute, is to sheer off; whereby one avoids, in like manner, either to give or take an affront: two things not much more to my mind the one than the t'other. And so, Madam, I wish you good day.'

He then, with a formal bow, left the room, Juliet gliding out by his side; while Mrs Howel, powerless to detain her, wreaked her pent-up wrath upon the bell, which she rang, till every waiter in the house came to hear, that she was now ready to set off for Chudleigh-park.

CHAPTER LXXXVIII

The kind looks, and determined approbation of the Admiral, gave Juliet, now, courage to address him with a petition for his advice, how she might arrive most expeditiously at Torbay.

'Torbay?' he repeated, 'why I could send you in my boat. But what,—' his brow overclouding, 'what has a modest girl to do at Torbay?'

Juliet answered, that she should join, there, a friend whom she meant to accompany to the continent.

Every mark of favour was now changed into disdainful displeasure; and, turning abruptly away from her, he muttered to himself, though aloud, that women's going abroad, to outlandish places, whereby they learnt more how to dizen themselves, and cut capers, than how to become good wives and mothers, was what he could not uphold; and would not lend a hand to; and then, without looking at her, he sullenly entered his own apartment.

The disappointed Juliet, utterly overset, was still dejectedly ruminating in the corridor, when she heard the servants of Mrs Howel announce, that their lady's carriage was ready.

She then recovered her feet, to escape any fresh offence by regaining her apartment.

Her situation appeared to her now to be as extraordinary, as it was sad and difficult. Entitled to an ample fortune, yet pennyless; indebted for her sole preservation from insult and from famine, to pecuniary obligations from accidental acquaintances, and those acquaintances, men! pursued, with documents of legal right, by one whom she shuddered to behold, and to whom she was so irreligiously tied, that she could not, even if she wished it, regard herself as his lawful wife; though so entangled, that her fetters seemed to be linked with duty and honour; unacknowledged,—perhaps disowned by her family; and, though born to a noble and yet untouched fortune, consigned to disguise, to debt, to indigence, and to flight!

While mournfully taking this review of her condition, and seeking, but vainly, to form some plan for its amelioration, she heard the potent voice of the Admiral call out, 'To Powderham Castle,' as a carriage drove from the house; but ere she had time to lament the mortifying errour of her benevolent, though ill judging friend, the approach to the door of some other vehicle, announced a fresh arrival; and, presently, all difficulties were absorbed in immediate terrour, as again she heard that sound, which, of all others, most severely shocked her nerves, the voice of Mrs Howel.

What could cause this abrupt return? Had she received the directions of Lord Denmeath? Was a new persecution arranged? or,—more horrible than all,— had means been devized, for casting again the most wretched of victims into the hands of the most terrific of her foes?

Tremblingly she listened to every noise. A general commotion, with quick pacing feet, spoke the entrance into the house of sundry servants; and, presently, she distinctly heard the apartment of Mrs Howel taken possession of by that lady, and by some person with whom she was discoursing.

All now, for about a quarter of an hour, was still. She was then alarmed by a rustling sound, and a single footstep in the corridor: it approached, stopt, seemed turning back; approached again; and, after a few minutes, she was startled by a tapping at her door.

She shook, she was all dismay and apprehension: she hesitated whether to bolt herself in, or to accord admission; but a second tap bringing to her reflection how short, how futile, how ineffectual would be any resistance, she turned the key, opened her door, and her room was instantly entered.

Often, in the course of her long struggles and difficulties, had Juliet been struck with astonishment; but never had she known surprize that could bear any comparison with that which she experienced at this moment; when, expecting to see Mrs Howel, or Lord Denmeath; when, prepared for reproach, for menace, and for insult; she saw, as fearfully she raised her eyes, instead of all that she dreaded and loathed, all that she thought most sweet, most lovely, most perfect upon earth, in the elegant form, and softly expressive face of Lady Aurora Granville, who, with eyes glistening, and arms opening, gently ejaculated, 'My sister!' and fell, weeping, upon her neck.

Juliet nearly ceased to breathe: wonder, yet incredulity, took possession of her faculties, and she knew not whether it were possible that this could be reality till the big surprize, mingled with the almost too powerful delight of her bosom, found some vent in a violent burst of tears.

Tender embraces, fond and open on the part of Lady Aurora, transported, yet fearful and doubtful, on that of Juliet, kept them for some minutes weeping in each other's arms. 'Can you, then,—' cried the penetrated Juliet,—'may I believe in such felicity?—Can you condescend so far as not to disdain,— disclaim,—and turn away from so unhappy a relation? so distressed,—so helpless,—so desolate an object?'

'Oh! hush! hush! hush!' cried Lady Aurora, putting her hand upon the mouth of Juliet; 'you must not break my heart by such an idea,—such a profanation!

by making me apprehend that you could ever think me such a monster! Did I wait till I knew your rights to my affection before I loved you? Did I not divine them from the moment I first conversed with you?'

Folding, then, her white arms around Juliet, with redoubled tenderness, 'Oh my sweet Miss Ellis!' she cried. 'Let me call you still a little while by that dear name! I have loved it so fondly that I can hardly love more even to call you my dearest sister! How you have engaged my thoughts; rested upon my imagination; occupied my ideas; been ever uppermost in my memory; and always highest,—Oh! higher than any one in my esteem and admiration! long, long before this loved moment, when Sir Jaspar Herrington's letter makes my enthusiasm but a tender duty!'

'Ah! Lady Aurora!' cried Juliet, 'what sufferings are not repaid by a moment such as this! by a blessing so superlative, as thus to be acknowledged, thus to be received, by the person whose virtues and whose sweetness would have made me delight in her favour, had I never wanted protection! had my lot in life been the most brilliant!'

'Oh hush! sweet sister, hush!' interrupted Lady Aurora, again stopping her mouth; 'what words are these? favour!—Lady Aurora!—Ah! never let me hear them more, if you love me! What have we to do with such phrases? Are we not sisters? Shall I use such to you? Would you love me if I did? Would you not rather chide me?'

Juliet could only shed tears, though tears so delicious, that it was luxury to shed them. Lady Aurora would have kissed them from her cheeks; but her own mingled with them so copiously, that it was not possible; and though the smiles of expressive joy that brightened each countenance, shewed their sensibility to be but fulness of happiness, the meeting, the acknowledgment, with the throbbing recollection of all that was passed, so touched each gentle heart, that they could but weep and embrace, embrace and weep, alternately.

'I have coveted,' at length cried Juliet, 'almost beyond light or life, I have coveted this precious moment! When first I heard you named,—you and Lord Melbury,—on the evening of the play, at Mrs Maple's, Oh! what were my emotions! my satisfaction, my apprehensions, my hopes, and my solicitude! When I saw two beings so sweet, so formed to create esteem and love, so innocent, so unassuming, so attractive,—and whispered to myself, Are these my nearest relations? Is this my sister? Is this my brother?—how did my heart expand with joy and pride! How did I long to cast off all disguise, all reserve, and cry Own me, amiable beings! sweet sister! loved brother! pure, kind, and good! own your unhappy sister! take to your pitying protection the distressed, persecuted, insulated daughter of your father!'

'Ah why,' cried Lady Aurora, 'did you not speak? why not indulge the impulse of nature, and of kindness? Your talents, your acquirements, your manners, won, instantly, all our admiration; enchanted, bewitched us; but how wide were we from thinking, at that first moment, that we had any tie to a mutual regard with the accomplished Miss Ellis! Our first notion of that happiness, though still far from the truth,—was after that cruel scene, which must for ever be blotted from all our memories;—when my poor brother was urged on,—so unhappily! to forget himself. The knowledge of that disgrace, from some listening servants, reached Mrs Howel; she communicated it to my uncle Denmeath: no wonder he was alarmed! Still, however, he told us not the story; though, to stop the progress of what he feared, he acquainted us, that a report had formerly been spread, that we had a distant relation abroad; not, he said,—forgive him, if possible!—not in a right line related, and never, by my father, meant to be any way acknowledged.—Oh how little he knew my father! or, let me say, either of his daughters!—But, having put my brother upon his guard, by suggesting that it was possible that you might be this distant and unhonoured relation.—Ah, my Miss Ellis! if you had seen our indignant looks, when we heard such phrases!—He promised to seek you himself, and to examine into the affair; and exacted, forced from us both a promise, in return, that we would never either meet or write to you, till he had ascertained what was the truth. The unfortunate scene at Mrs Howel's alone made my brother submit; for he feared misconstruction: and his submission of course included mine. Ah! had you spoken at that time! had you revealed—'

'Alas! my distresses were so complicate! What most I wished upon earth, was constantly counteracted by what most I dreaded! I could not make myself known to my friends,—in the soothing supposition that such I should find!—without betraying myself to my enemy; for Lord Denmeath would assuredly have made me over to my persecutor. How, then, in a situation so critical, yet so helpless, could I selfishly involve in my wretchedness, my perplexity and my concealment, the kindest and tenderest of human hearts?'

'Frequently,' said Lady Aurora, 'we have considered, and consulted together, what steps we ought to take; but the fear of some mistake, some imprudence, some offence, in a point so doubtful, so delicate, made us always decide that it was for you to speak first. And when I pressed so earnestly for your confidence, it was in the hope, the flattering hope, that I should prove my title to taking such a liberty. I had not, else, been so importunate, so inconsiderate. My brother, too, actuated by the same hope, urged you, perhaps, even more precipitately; but in all honour, with all respect; with no view, no thought, but to cement our regard by the ties of kindred. My brother can scarcely yet know our beloved acquisition; but Sir Jaspar tells me that he has sent a duplicate-letter to him, with the same precious history that he has written to me. Oh, how fervent will be his delight!'

She then related, to the grateful, but joy overpowered Juliet, that she had herself but just acquired this information, through the letter of which she had spoken; and which had been put into her hands, as she was setting out for Chudleigh-park; to which place Mrs Howel had, hastily, asked her to set off first, with her maid; promising to overtake her by the way.

The letter from Sir Jaspar, Lady Aurora continued, changed the whole system of her conduct. When she learnt that Miss Ellis, instead of being either an adventurer, or a distant and unhonoured relation, was the daughter of her own father; by a first, a lawful, though a secret marriage; all difficulty and irresolution vanished. Her first duty, she now thought, was the duty of a daughter, in the acknowledgment of a sister.

She gave orders that her chaise should be driven back instantly to Teignmouth; but, before she reached that village, she met Mrs Howel; with whose woman she immediately changed place; and then communicated the interesting intelligence that she had just received. Mrs Howel was utterly confounded; having either never conceived the truth, or been of opinion, with Lord Denmeath, that the interest, and the dignity of his lordship's nephew and niece, demanded its disavowal, or concealment. But when Lady Aurora openly protested, that she must instantly address her sister, through the medium of Sir Jaspar Herrington; Mrs Howel, to stop any written acknowledgment, confessed that the young person was at Teignmouth; earnestly, however, insisting that no measure should be adopted, till the arrival of Lord Denmeath, to whom she had already sent an express. But Lady Aurora no sooner heard this welcome news, than, stimulated by conceiving, that her inclinations and her sense of right, were now one, she grew inflexible in her turn; and resolved to acknowledge and embrace her sister, without any other permission than the law of nature. Mrs Howel, conscious, Lady Aurora thought, that, should the business take a new turn, from the interference of Sir Jaspar Herrington, she might, already, have gone too far, was fain to accompany her back to the lodging-house; and, after giving many admonitions, to submit to the irrepressible impatience which sunk the niece in the sister.

Lady Aurora solicited, now, to know for what reason the name of Ellis had been taken; and learnt that, in the terrible perturbation in which Juliet had parted from the Marchioness, they had hastily agreed upon two initial letters for their correspondence; reserving some better adoption to a consultation with Gabriella. To have used the name of Granville, would have been courting danger and pursuit. But the embarrassed avowal of Juliet, that had been surprized from her at Dover, by the abrupt interrogatory of Elinor, that she knew not, herself, what she ought to be called; stood, ever after, in the way of any regulation upon that difficult point. She had been glad, therefore, to subscribe to the blunder of Miss Bydel, which seemed, in some measure, retaining an appellation, at least a sound, designed for her by the Marchioness; and which could not be called a deception, since all who then knew her, knew, also, its origin.

Lady Aurora acknowledged, that, even from their childhood, both Lord Melbury and herself had heard, though secretly and vaguely, of a suspected elder born; but not of a prior marriage; and they had often wished to meet with Miss Powel; for calumny and mystery, while they had hidden the truth, had not concealed the attachment of Lord Granville, nor the suspicious disappearance of its object, and her mother.

Innumerable plans, now, varying and short lived, because unsanctioned by any authority, succeeded to one another, of what measures might be adopted for their living together immediately. 'For how,' cried Juliet, 'could I, henceforth, sustain an insulated life? How bear to look around me, again, and see no one whose kindness I could claim? Oh, how support so forlorn a state, after feeling every sorrow subside on the bosom,—may I, indeed, say so?— on the loved bosom of a sister?'

Thus, in the grateful transports of sensations as exquisite as they were sudden and unexpected, Juliet, acknowledged as her sister by Lady Aurora Granville; and with hopes all alive of the tender protection of a brother, felt every pulse, once again, beat to happiness; while every fear and foreboding, though not annihilated, was set aside.

CHAPTER LXXXIX

While time was yet a stranger to regulation, and ere the dial shewed its passage; when it had no computation but by our feelings, our weariness, our occupations, or our passions; the sun which arose splendid upon felicity, must have excited, by its quick parting rays, a surprise nearly incredulous; while that which gave light but to sorrow, may have appeared, at its evening setting, to have revolved the whole year. This period, so long past, seemed now present to Lady Aurora and to Juliet; so uncounted flew the minutes; so unconscious were they that they had more than met, more than embraced, more than reciprocated their joy in acknowledged kindred; that each felt amazed as well as shocked, when a summons from Mrs Howel to Lady Aurora, told them that the day was fast wearing, away.

Lady Aurora reluctantly obeyed the call; and in thanksgiving, pious and delighted, Juliet spent the interval of her absence.

It was not long; she returned precipitately; but colourless, trembling, and altered, though making an effort to smile: but the struggle against her feelings ended in a burst of tears; and, again falling upon the neck of Juliet; 'Oh my sweet sister!' she cried, 'is your persecution never to end?'

Juliet, though quickly alarmed, fondly answered, 'It is over already! While that precious appellation comes from your lips,—sweet title of tenderness and affection!—I feel above every danger!'

Lady Aurora, bitterly weeping, was compelled, then, to acknowledge that she had been hurried away by Mrs Howel, to be told that a foreigner, ill dressed, and just arrived from the Continent, was demanding, in broken English, of every one that he met, some news of a young person called Miss Ellis.

The exaltation of Juliet was instantly at an end; and, in an accent of despair, she uttered, 'Is it so soon, then, over!—my transient felicity!'

Whether this foreigner were her persecutor himself, escaped and disguised; or some emissary employed to claim or to entrap her, was all of doubt by which she was momentarily supported; for she felt as determined to resist an agent, as she thought herself incapable to withstand the principal.

Mrs Howel, who had heard of the search, represented to Lady Aurora, the extreme impropriety of her ladyship's intercourse with a person thus suspiciously pursued; at least till the opinion of Lord Denmeath could be known. But Lady Aurora, fully satisfied that this helpless fugitive was her half-sister, was now as firm as she had hitherto been facile; and declared that, though her personal inclinations should still yield to her respect for her uncle, her sense of filial duty to the memory of her father, must bind her, openly and unreservedly, to sustain his undoubted daughter.

A waiter now interrupted them, to demand admission to Miss Ellis for a foreigner.

'She is not here!—There is no Miss Ellis here! No such person!'— precipitately cried Lady Aurora; but the foreigner himself, who stood behind the waiter, glided into the room.

Lady Aurora nearly fainted; Juliet screamed and hid her face; the foreigner called out, 'Ah Mademoiselle Juliette! c'est, donc, vous! et vous ne me reconnoissez pas?'[14]

'Ah heaven!' cried Juliet, uncovering her face; 'Ambroise! my good, my excellent Ambroise! is it you?—and you only?'—Turning then, enraptured, to Lady Aurora, 'Kindest,' she cried, 'and tenderest of human beings! condescend to receive, and to aid me to thank, the valuable person to whom I owe my first deliverance!'

Lady Aurora, revived and charmed, poured forth the warmest praises; while Juliet, eagerly demanding news of the Marchioness; and whether he could give any intelligence of the Bishop; saw his head droop, and seized with terrour, exclaimed, 'Oh Ambroise! am I miserable for ever!'

He hastened to assure her that they were both alive, and well; and, in the ecstacy of her gratitude, upon the cessation of her first direful surmise, she promised to receive all other information with courage.

He shook his head, with an air the most sorrowful; and then related that the Bishop, after delays, dangers, fruitless journies, and disasters innumerable, which had detained him many months in the interiour, had, at last, and most unfortunately, reached a port, whence he was privately to embark for joining his niece, just as the commissary, upon returning from his abortive expedition, was re-landed. By some cruel accident, the voice of the prelate reached his ear: immediate imprisonment, accompanied by treatment the most ignominious, ensued. Ambroise, who, for the satisfaction of the Marchioness, had attended the Bishop to the coast, was seized also; and both would inevitably have been executed, had not a project occurred to the commissary, of employing Ambroise to demand and recover his prey, and her dowry.

Ambroise stopt and wept.

Bloodless now became the face of Juliet, though with forced, yet decided courage, 'I understand you!' she cried, 'and Oh! if I can save him,—by any sacrifice, any devotion,—I am contented! and I ought to be happy!'

'Ah, cruel sister!' cried Lady Aurora; 'would you kill me?'—

Juliet, shedding a torrent of tears, tenderly embraced her.

'The Bishop,' Ambroise continued, 'no sooner comprehended than he forbade the attempt; but he was consigned, unheard, to a loathsome cell; and Ambroise was almost instantly embarked; with peremptory orders to acquaint *la citoyenne Julie* that unless she returned immediately to her husband, in order to sign and seal, by his side, and as his wife, their joint claim to her portion, upon the terms that Lord Denmeath had dictated; the most tremendous vengeance should fall upon the hypocritical old priest, by every means the most terrible that could be devised.'

'I am ready! quite ready!' cried the pale Juliet, with energy; 'I do not sacrifice, I save myself by preserving my honoured guardian!'

This eagerness to rescue her revered benefactor, which made her feel gloriously, though transiently, the exaltation of willing martyrdom, soon subsided into the deepest grief, upon seeing Lady Aurora, shivering, speechless, and nearly lifeless, sink despondingly upon the ground.

Juliet, kneeling by her side, and pressing her nearly cold face to her bosom, bathed her cheeks, throat, and shoulders with fast falling tears; but felt incapable of changing her plan. Yet all her own anguish was almost intolerably embittered, by thus proving the fervour of an affection, in which almost all her wishes might have been concentrated, but that honour, conscience, and religion united to snatch her from its enjoyment.

The news that Lady Aurora was taken ill, spread quickly to Mrs Howel; and brought that lady to the apartment of Juliet in person. Lady Aurora was already recovered, and seated in the folding arms of Juliet, with whom her tears were bitterly, but silently mingling.

Mrs Howel, shocked and alarmed, summoned the female attendants to conduct her ladyship to her own apartment.

Lady Aurora would accept no aid save from Juliet; fondly leaning upon whose arm she reached a sofa in her bed-chamber; where she assumed, though with cruel struggles against her yielding nature, voice and courage to pronounce, 'My dear Mrs Howel, you have always been so singularly good to me,—you have always done me so much honour, that you must not, will not refuse to be kinder to me still, and to permit me to introduce to you ... Miss Granville!... For this young lady, Mrs Howel, is my sister!... my very dear sister!'

Utterly confounded, Mrs Howel made a silent inclination of the head, with eyes superciliously cast down. The letter of Sir Jaspar Herrington had not failed to convince her that this was the real offspring of Lord Granville; whose existence had never been doubted in the world, but whose legitimacy had never been believed. Still, however, Mrs Howel, who was now, from her own hard conduct, become the young orphan's personal enemy, flattered herself that means might be found to prevent the publication of such a story; and determined to run no risk by appearing to give it credit; at the same time that, in her uncertainty of the event, she softened the austerity of her manner; and gave orders to the servants to shew every possible respect to a person who had the honour to be admitted to Lady Aurora Granville.

Juliet was in too desperate a state for any thought, or care, relative to Mrs Howel; and, having soothed Lady Aurora by promises of a speedy return, she hastened back to Ambroise.

She earnestly besought him, since her decision would be immutable, to make immediate enquiries whence they might embark with the greatest expedition.

Sadly, yet, so circumstanced, not unwillingly he agreed; and gave to her aching heart nearly the only joy of which it was susceptible, in the news that the Marchioness was already at the sea-side, awaiting the expected arrival of her darling daughter.

Ambroise had been entrusted, he said, by the commissary, with this cruel office, from his well known fidelity to the Marchioness and to the Bishop, which, where the alternative was so dreadful, would urge him, whatever might be his repugnance, to its faithful discharge. His orders had been to proceed straight to Salisbury, whence, under the name of Miss Ellis, he was to seek Juliet in every direction. And her various adventures had made so much noise in that neighbourhood, that she had been traced, with very little difficulty to Teignmouth.

Her terrible compliance being thus solemnly fixed, she left him to prepare for their departure the next morning, and returned to the afflicted Lady Aurora; by whose side she remained till midnight; struggling to sink her own sufferings, and to hide her shuddering disgust and horrour, in administering words of comfort, and exhibiting an example of fortitude, to her weeping sister.

But when, early the next morning, with the dire idea of leave-taking, she re-visited the gentle mourner, she found her nourishing a hope that her Juliet might yet be melted to a change of plan. 'Oh my sister!' she cried, 'my whole heart cannot thus have been opened to affection, to confidence, to fondest friendship, only to be broken by this dreadful separation! Our souls cannot have been knit together by ties of the sweetest trust, only to be rent for ever asunder! You will surely reflect before you destroy us both? for do you think you can now be a single victim?'

Dissolved with tenderness, yet agonized with grief, Juliet could but weep, and ejaculate half-pronounced blessings; while Lady Aurora, with renovating courage, said, 'Ah! think, sweet Juliet, think, if our father,—was he not ours alike?—had lived to know the proud day of receiving his long lost, and so accomplished daughter, such as I see her now!—would he not have said to me, 'Aurora! this is your sister! You are equally my children; love her, then, tenderly, and let there be but one heart between you!'—And will you, then, Juliet, deliver us both up to wretchedness? Must I see you no more? And only have seen you, now, to embitter all the rest of my life?'

'Oh resistless Aurora!' cried the miserable Juliet, 'rend not thus my heart!—Think for me, my Aurora;—Think, as well as feel for me,—and then—dispose of me as you will!'—

'I accept being the umpire, my Juliet! my tenderest sister! I accept it, and you are saved!—We are both saved!—for this would be a sacrifice beyond any call of duty!'—cried Lady Aurora, instantly reviving, not simply to serenity, but to felicity, to rapture. Her tears were dried up, her eyes shone with delight, and smiles the softest and most expressive dimpled her chin, and played about her cheeks and mouth, while, with a transport new to her serene temperament, she embraced the appalled Juliet. ''Tis now, indeed,' she continued, 'I feel I have a sister! 'Tis now I feel the force of kindred fondness! If you had not loved me with a sister's affection, you would not have listened to my solicitations; and if you had not listened, such a disappointment, and your loss together,—do you think I should have been strong enough to survive them?' But this enchantment lasted not long; she soon perceived it was without participation, and her joy vanished, 'like the baseless fabric of a vision.' Anguish sat upon the brow of Juliet; fits of shuddering horrour shook every limb; and her only answer to these tender endearments was by tears and embraces; while she strove to hide her altered and nearly distorted face upon Lady Aurora's shoulder.

'Speak to me, my sister!' cried Lady Aurora. 'Tell me that your pity for the good Bishop is not stronger than all your love for me? than all your value for your own security from barbarous brutality? than your trust in Providence, that will surely protect so pious and exemplary a person?'

'No, Heaven forbid!' answered Juliet; 'but, when Providence permits us to see a way,—when it opens a path to us by which evil may be avoided, by which duty may be exerted,—ought the difficulties of that way, the perils of that path, to make us recoil from the attempt? When the natural means are obvious, ought we to wait for some miracle?'

'Ah, my sister!' cried Lady Aurora, 'would you, then, still go? Have you yielded in mere transient compassion?'

'No, sweet Aurora, no! To ruin your peace would every way destroy Mine! Yet—what a fatality! to fear the very enjoyment of the family protection for which I have been sighing my whole life, lest I can enjoy it but by a crime! I abandon the post of honour, in leaving the benefactor, the supporter, the preserver of my orphan existence, to perpetual chains, if not to massacre!—Or I break the tender heart of the gentlest, purest, and most beloved of sisters!'

Lady Aurora, now, looked all consternation; and, after a disturbed pause, 'If you think it wrong,' she cried, 'not to sacrifice yourself,—Oh my sister! let not mere commiseration for my weakness lead you astray! We all know there is another world, in which we yet may meet again!'

'Angel! angel!' cried Juliet, pressing Lady Aurora to her bosom. 'You will aid me, then, to do right' by nobly supporting yourself, you will help to keep me from sinking? Religion will give you strength of mind to submit to our worldly separation, and all my sufferings will be endurable, while they open to me the hope of a final re-union with my angel sister!'

They now mutually sought to re-animate each other. Piety strengthened the fortitude of Juliet, and supplied its place to Lady Aurora; and, in soft pity to each other, each strove to look away from, and beyond, all present and actual evil; and to work up their minds, by religious hopes and reflections, to an enthusiastic foretaste of the joys of futurity.

CHAPTER XC

This tenderly touching intercourse was broken in upon by a summons to Ambroise, whom Juliet found waiting for her in the corridor; where he was beginning to recount to her, that he had met with a sea-officer, who had promised him a letter of recommendation for procuring a passport, if he could bring proof that he was a proper person for having one; when the Admiral issued abruptly from his apartment.

He took off his hat, though with a severe air, to Juliet, who, abashed, passed on to her chamber; but stopping and bluffly accosting Ambroise, 'Harkee!' he cried, 'my lad! a word with you!—Pray, what business have you with that girl? I have, I know, as good as promised to help you off; but let all be fair and above board. I don't pretend to have much taste for any person who would go out of old England when once he has got footing into it; thoff if I had had the misfortune to be born in France, there's no being sure that I might not have liked it myself; from knowing no better: for which reason I think nothing narrower than holding a man cheap for loving his country, be it ever so bad a one. Therefore, if you have a mind, my lad, as far as yourself goes, to sheer off; as you are neither a sailor nor a soldier, nor, moreover, a prisoner, I will lend you a hand and welcome. But no foul play! If there's any person of your acquaintance, that, after being born in old England, wants to go flaunting and jiggetting to outlandish countries, you'll do well to give her a hint to keep astern of me; for I shall never uphold a person who behaves o' that sort.'

Ambroise, in broken English, earnestly entreated him not to withdraw his promised protection; and Juliet, desirous to obtain his counsel for the execution of her perilous enterprize, ventured back, and joined to petition for instructions where she might embark most expeditiously; endeavouring to make her peace with him, by solemnly avowing, that necessity, not inclination, urged her to undertake this voyage; and claiming assistance, a second time, from his tried benevolence.

The words tried benevolence, and a second time, which inadvertently escaped her, from eagerness to interest his attention, struck him forcibly with ire. 'Avast!' he cried, 'none of your flummery! You think, belike, because you've got a pretty face, to make a fool of me? but that's sooner thought than done! You'll excuse me for speaking my mind a little plainly; for how the devil, asking your pardon for such a word, should I do any thing for you a second time, when I have never seen or thought of you, up to this moment, a first? Please to tell me that!'

Juliet, looking round, and seeing that no witnesses were by, gently enquired whether he had no remembrance of a poor voyager, whom he had had the charity to save, the preceding winter, from immediate destruction, by admitting into a boat?

'What! a swarthy minx? with a sooty sort of skin, and all over rags and jags? Yes, yes, I remember her well enough: I thank her! but I don't much advise her to come in my way! She turned out a mere impostor. She was probably French. I gave her a guinea, and paid for her place to town, and her entertainment. She took my guinea, and eat and drank; and then made off by some other way! and has never been heard of since. I described her at all the Dover stages and diligences; for I intended to give her a trifle more, to help her to find her friends, for fear of her falling into bad hands. But I could never get any tidings of her; she was a mere cheat. How did you come to know the jade?'

Juliet blushed violently, and, with some difficulty stammered out, 'Kind as you are, Sir, good and charitable,—you have not well judged that young person!'—

'By all that's sacred,' cried he, striking his cane upon the ground, 'if it were possible for a girl to be painted to such a pitch of nicety, I should swear you were that very mamselle yourself!—though, if you are, I should take it as a favour if you would tell me, how the devil it came into your head to let me pay for your stage-coach, when you never made use of your place? Where the fun of that was I can't make out!'

'I am but too sensible, Sir, that every thing seems against me!' said Juliet, in a melancholy tone; 'yet the time, probably, is not very far off, when I may be able sufficiently to explain myself, to cause you much regret,—so generous seems your nature;—should you refuse me your services in my very great distress!'

The Admiral now looked deeply perplexed, yet evidently touched. 'I should be loath, Madam,' he said, 'very loath, indeed, for the matter of that, there's something so agreeable in you,—to think you no better than you should be. Not that one ought to expect perfection; for a woman is but a woman; which a man, as her native superiour, ought always to keep in mind; however, don't take it amiss that I throw out that remark; for I don't mean it to dash you.'

Juliet, too much shocked to reply, cast up her eyes in silent appeal to heaven, and, entering her room, resolved to fold two guineas in a small packet, and to send them to the Admiral by Ambroise, for an immediate acquittal of her double pecuniary debt.

But the Admiral, struck by her manner, looked thoughtful, and dissatisfied with himself; and, again calling to Ambroise, said, 'Harkee, my lad! I should not be sorry to know who that young gentlewoman is?—I am afraid she thinks me rather unmannerly. And the truth is, I don't know that I have been over and above polite: which I take shame to myself for, I give you my word; for I am always devilish bad company with myself when I have misbehaved to a female; because why? She has no means to right herself. So I beg you to make my excuse to the gentlewoman. And please to tell her that, though I am no great friend to ceremony, I am very sorry if I have affronted her.'

Ambroise said, that he was sure the young lady would think no more of it, if his honour would but be kind enough to give the recommendatory letter.

'Why, with regard to that,' said the Admiral, after some deliberation, 'I would do her any service, whereby I might shew my good will; after having been rather over-rough, be her class what it may, considering she's a female; and, moreover, seems somewhat in jeopardy; if I were not so cursedly afraid of being put upon! You, that are but an outlandish man,—though I can't say but you've as good a look as another man;—a very honest look, if one might judge by the face;—which made me take to you, without much thinking what I was about, I can tell you!—'

Ambroise, bowing low, hoped that he would not repent his goodness.

'You, I say, being more in the use of being juggled, begging your pardon, from its being more the custom of foreign parts; can have no great notion, naturally, how little a British tar,—a person you don't know over-much about, I believe!' smiling, 'there not being a great many such, as I am told, off our own shores!—You, as I was remarking, can't be expected to have much notion how little a British tar relishes being over-reached. But the truth, Sir, is, we are set afloat upon the wide ocean, before we have well done with our slabbering bibs; which makes us the men we are! But, then, all we know of the world is only by bits and scraps; except, mayhap, what we can pick out of books. And that's no great matter; for the chief of a seaman's library is most commonly the history of cheats and rogues; so that we are always upon the look out, d'ye see, for fear of false colours.'

Ambroise began a warm protestation of his honesty.

'Not but that, let me tell you, Sir!' the Admiral went on, 'we have as many good scholars upon quarter-deck, counting such as could pay for their learning when they were younkers, as in any other calling. But this was not the case with myself, who owe nothing to birth nor favour; whereof I am proud to be thankful; for, from ten years old, when I was turned adrift by my family, I have had little or no schooling,—except by the buffets of the world.'

Then, after ruminating for some minutes, he told Ambroise that he should not be sorry to make his apologies to the gentlewoman himself; adding, 'For I could have sworn, when I first met her in the gallery, I had seen her some where before; though I could not make out how nor when. But if she's only that black madmysell washed white, I should like to have a little parley with her. She may possibly do me the service of helping me to find a friend; and if she does, I sha'n't be backward, God willing, to requite her. And harkee, my lad! I should be glad to know the gentlewoman's name. What's she called?'

'She's called Mademoiselle Juliette, Monsieur.'

'Juliet?—Are you sure of that?' cried the Admiral, starting. 'Juliet?—Are you very sure, Sir?'

'Oui, oui, Monsieur.'

'Harkee, sirrah! if you impose upon me, I'll trounce you within an inch of your life! Juliet, do you say? Are you sure it's Juliet?'

'Oui, Monsieur; Mademoiselle Juliette.'

'Why then, as I am a living man, and on this side t'other world, I must speak to her directly! Tell her so this instant.'

Ambroise tapped, and Juliet opened the door; but, when he would have spoken, the Admiral, taking him by the shoulders, and turning him round, bid him go about his business; and, entering the room, shut the door, and flung himself upon a chair.

Rising, however, almost at the same instant, though much agitated, he made sundry bows, but tried vainly to speak; while the astonished Juliet waited gravely for some explanation of so strange an intrusion.

'Madam,' he at length said, 'that Frenchman there,—who, it's like enough, don't know what he says,—pretends your name is Juliet?'

'Sir!'—

'If it be so, Ma'am,—you'll do me a remarkable piece of service, if you will be so complaisant as to let me know how you came by that name?'

Juliet now felt alarmed.

'It's rather making free, Ma'am, I confess, but I shall take it as a special favour, if you'll be pleased to tell me what part of the world you come from?'

'Sir, I—I—'

'If you think my inquisitiveness impertinent, Ma'am; which it's like enough you may, I shall beg leave to give you an item of my reason for it; and then it's odds but you'll make less scruple to give me the reply. Not that I mean to make conditions; for binding people down only hampers good will. But when you have heard me, you may be glad, perchance, to speak of your own accord; for I don't know, I give you my solemn word, but that at this very moment you are talking to one of your own kin!'

He fixed his eyes upon her, then, with great earnestness.

'My own kin?—What, Sir, do you mean?'

'I'll tell you out of hand, Ma'am,—if I may be so bold as to sit down; for whether we happen to be relations or no', there can be no law against our being friends.'

Juliet hastily presented him a chair, and scarcely breathed from eagerness to reciprocate the enquiry. She had never heard the Admiral mentioned but by his military title.

Seated now by her side, he looked at her for some instants, smilingly, though with glistening eyes; 'Madam,' he said, 'I had a sister whose name was Juliet! —and the name is dear to my soul for her sake! And it's no common name; so that I never hear it without being moved. She left a child, Ma'am, who for some unnatural reasons, that I sha'n't enter upon just now, was brought up in foreign parts. This child had her own sweet name; and her own sweet character, too, I make small doubt; as well as her own sweet face.'—

He stopt, and again more earnestly looked at Juliet; but, seeing her strongly affected, begged her pardon, and, brushing a tear from his eye, went on.

'When I came home from my last station in the East Indies, I crossed over the channel to see after her; a great proof of my good will, I can tell you! for no little thing would have carried me to that lawless place; and from the best land upon God's earth! but I got nothing for my pains, except a cursed bad piece of news, which turned me upside down; for I was told that she was married to a French monsieur! Upon which I swore, God willing, never to see her face to the longest day I had to live! And I came away with that resolution. However, a Christian is never so perfect himself, as not to look over a flaw in his neighbour. Wherefore, if I could get any item of the poor girl's repentance, I don't think, for my dear sister's sake, but I could still take her to my bosom, —yea, to my very heart of hearts!'

'Tell me, Sir,' cried Juliet, rising, with clasped hands, and eyes fast filling with tears; 'tell me,—for I have never heard it,—your name?'

'By all that's holy!' cried he, rising too, and trembling, 'you make my heart beat all over my body!—My name is Powel! In the name, then, of the Most High,—are you not my niece yourself?'

Juliet dropt at his feet; 'Oh heavenly Providence!' she ejaculated, 'you are then my poor mother's brother!' Speech now, for a considerable time, was denied to both; strong emotions, though of joy, nearly suffocated Juliet, while the Admiral sobbed over her as he pressed her in his arms.

'My girl!' he cried, when a little recovered, 'my sister's daughter!—daughter of the dearest of sisters!—I have found, then, at last, something appertaining to my poor sister! You shall be dear to my soul for her sake, whatever you may be for your own. And, moreover, as to what you may have done up to this time, whereof I don't mean to judge uncharitably, every one of us being but frail, I shall let it all pass by. So hold up your head, and take comfort, my girl, and don't be shy of your old uncle; for whatever may have slipt from him in a moment of choler, he'll protect you, God willing, to his last hour; and never come out with another unkind word upon what is past and gone.'

The heart of Juliet was too full to let her offer any immediate vindication: she could but pronounce, 'My uncle, when I can be explicit,—you will not—I hope, and trust,—have cause to blush for me!'—

'Why then you are a very good girl!' cried he, well pleased, 'an excellent girl, in the main, I make small doubt.' He then demanded, though not, he protested, to find fault with what was past; what had brought her over to her native land in such a ragged, mauled, and black condition; which had prevented the least guess of who she was; 'for if, when I saw you off the coast,' he continued, 'you had shewn yourself such as you are now, you have so strong a look of my dear sister, that I should have hailed you out of hand. Though when I saw you Here it never came into my head; because why? I believed you to be There. And yet, instinct is main powerful, whereof I am a proof; for I took a fancy to you, even when I thought you an old woman; and, which is worse, a French woman. Coming away from those shores gave me a good opinion of you at once.'

He then made many tender enquiries concerning the last illness, and the death of Mrs Powel, his mother; whom it was now, he said, one-and-twenty years since he had seen; as, upon his poor father's insolvency, he had been taken from the royal navy, and sent out, in the company's service, to the East Indies.

Juliet, after satisfying his filial solicitude, ventured to express her own, upon every circumstance of her mother's life, which had fallen to his knowledge.

The insolvency, the Admiral replied, had soon been succeeded by the death of his father; and then his poor mother and sister had been driven to a cheap country residence, in the neighbourhood of Melbury-Hall. There, before he set out for the East Indies, he had passed a few days to take leave; in which time Lord Granville, the Earl of Melbury's only son, who had met them, it seems, in their rural strolls, had got such a footing in their house, that he called in both morning and evening; and stayed sometimes for hours, without knowing how time went. Uneasy upon remarking this, he counselled his sister to keep out of the young nobleman's way; and advised his mother to change her house. They both promised so to do; but, for all that, before he set sail, he determined to wait upon his lordship himself; which he did accordingly; and made free to tell him, that he should take it but kind of his lordship, if he would not be quite so sweet upon his sister. His lordship made fair promises, with such a genteelness, that there was no help but to give him credit; and, this being done, he went off with an easy heart. He remained in the Company's service some time; during which, the letters of his mother brought him the sorrowful tidings of his sister's death; followed up, afterwards, by an account that, for her own health's sake, she was gone over to reside in France.

'This was a bit of news,' he continued, 'which I did not take quite so kindly as I ought, mayhap, to have done, it not appertaining to a son to have the upper hand of his mother. But, having been, from the first, somewhat of a spoilt child, whereby my poor mother made herself plenty of trouble; I was always rather over choleric when I was contradicted. Taking it, therefore, rather amiss her going out of old England, no great matter of letter-writing passed between us from that time, to my return to my native land.

'It was then I was told the worst tiding that ever I wish to hear! one came, and t'other came, and all had some fuel to make the fire burn fiercer, to give me an item that Lord Granville had over-persuaded my sister to elope with him; and that she died of a broken heart; leaving a child, that my mother, for my sister's reputation's sake, had gone to bring up in foreign parts. My blood boiled so, then, in my veins, that how it ever got cool enough not to burn me to a cinder is a main wonder. But I vowed revenge, and that, I take it, sustained me; revenge being, to my seeming, a noble passion, when it is not to spite those who have done an ill turn to ourselves, but to punish those who have oppressed the helpless. What aggravated me the more, was hearing that he was married; and had two fine children, who were dawdled about every day in his coach; while the child of my poor sister was shut up, immured, no body knew where, in an outlandish country. I called him, therefore, to account, and bid him meet me, at five o'clock in the morning, at a coffee-house. We went into a private room. I used no great matter of ceremony in coming to the point. You have betrayed, I cried, the unprotected! You have seduced the forlorn! You have sold yourself to the devil!—and as you have given him, of your own accord, your soul, I am come to lend a hand to your giving him your body.'—

'Shocking!—Shocking!' interrupted Juliet. 'O my uncle!'—

'Why it was not over mannerly, I own; but I was too much aggrieved to stand upon complimenting. I loved her, said I, with all my heart and soul; but I bore patiently with her death, because I am a Christian; and I know that life and death come from God; but I scorn to bear with her dishonour, for that comes from a man. For the sake of your wife and children, as they are not in fault, I would conceal your unmanly baseness; but for the sake of my much injured sister, who was dearer to me than all your kin and kind, I intend, by the grace, and with the help of the Most High, to take a proper vengeance for her wrongs, by blowing out your brains; unless, by the law of chance, you should blow out mine; which, however, I should hold myself the most pitiful of cowards to expect in so just a cause.

'I then presented him my pistols, and gave him his choice which he would have.'

'Oh my poor father!' cried Juliet. 'Go on, my uncle, go on!'

'He heard me to the finish without a word; and with a countenance so sad, yet so firm, and which had so little the hue of guilt, that I have thought since, many a time and often, that, if choler had not blinded me, I should have stopt half way, and said, This is purely an innocent man!'

'Oh blessed be that word!' cried Juliet, clasping her hands, 'and blessed, blessed be my uncle for so kindly pronouncing it!'

'With what temper he answered me! If I insisted, he said, upon satisfaction, he would not deny it me; "And I ought, indeed," he said, "after an attack so insulting, to demand it for myself. But you are in an errour; and your cause seems so completely the cause of justice and virtue, that I cannot defend, till I have cleared myself. The sister whom you would avenge was the beloved of my soul! Never will you mourn for her as I have mourned! I neither betrayed nor seduced her. The love that I bore her was as untainted as her own honour. The immoveable views of my father to another alliance, kept our connexion secret; but your sister, your unspotted sister, was my wedded wife!"—The joy of my heart, at that moment, my dear girl, made me forget all my mishaps. I jumped,—for I was but a boy, then, to what I am now; and I flung my arms about his neck, and kissed him; which his lordship did not seem to take at all unkindly. Since she is not dishonoured, I cried, I can bear all else like a man. She is gone, indeed, my poor sister!—but 'tis to heaven she is gone! and I can but pray that we may both, in our due time, go there after her!—And upon that,—if I were to tell you the honest truth,—we both fell a blubbering.—But she was no common person, my dear sister!'

Juliet wept with varying emotions.

'His lordship,' the Admiral continued, 'then recorded the whole history of his marriage, the birth of his child, and the loss of his poor wife. That the child, accompanied by her grandmother, who scarcely breathed out of its sight, was gone to be brought up in a convent, under the care of a family of quality, that had a grand castle in its neighbourhood; and under the immediate guidance of a worthy old parson; that, as soon as she was educated, he should go over to fetch her, and write a letter to his father to own his first marriage. But he begged me, for family-reasons, to agree to the concealment, till I returned home for good; and had a house of my own in which I could receive the child, in the case his second lady and his father should behave unhandsomely. I had no great taste for a hiding scheme; but I was so overcome with joy to think my sister had been always a woman of honour, that I was in no cue for squabbling: and, moreover, I gave way with the greater complaisance, from the fear of seeing the child fall into the hands of people who would be ashamed of her, whereby her spirit might be broken; and, moreover, I can't say but I took it kind of his lordship the thought of letting her come to a house of mine; for I had already returned to his majesty's service; which, God willing, the devil himself shall never draw me from again; and I was a post-captain, and in pretty good circumstances. So I thought I had as well not meddle, nor do mischief. And the more, as his lordship was so honourable as to entrust to me a copy of a codicil to his will; written all in his own hand, and duly signed and sealed; wherein he owns his lawful marriage with my poor sister; and leaves her child the same fortune that he leaves to his daughters by his wife of quality.'

'Is it possible!—How fortunate! And have you, still, my dear uncle, this codicil?'

'Have I? Aye, my girl! I would sooner part with my right hand! It's the proof and declaration of my sister's honour! and I would not change it against all the diamonds, and all the pearls, and all the shawls of all the nabobs of all Asia! It has been my whole comfort in all my difficult voyages and hard services.'

Ah! thought Juliet, were my revered Bishop safe, I might now be every way happy!

'What passed in my mind at that time, was to cross over the Channel, to get my dear mother's blessing, and to give my own to my little niece. But it's of no great consequence what we plan, if it is not upheld by the Most High. I was all prepared, but I wrote never a word over, for the sake of giving my mother a surprize; when, all at once, I had a sudden promotion, with orders to return to the East Indies. And there I was stationed, on and off, in and out, till t'other day, as one may say. And when, at last, I got home again; meaning to marry Jenny Barker,—as pretty a girl as ever came into the world; and to set her at the head of my house, and equip her handsomely,—I found every thing turned upside down! Lord Granville had been dead five months, and his father about as many weeks. I had already heard, in the Indies, that my poor mother was dead; and when I went to get a little comfort with Jenny Barker, and to give her the baubles I had got together for her in the Indies,—always priding myself in thinking how smart she'd look in this! and how pretty her face would peep out of that!—I found her so mortally changed, that I took her for her own mother! who I had left to the full as well looking twenty years before; for, after my first voyage, by ill luck, I had not seen Jenny, who was down in the country.'

'But if she is amiable, uncle, and worthy—'

'You have a right way of thinking, my dear; and I honour you for it: but the disappointment came upon me so slap-dash, as one may say, for want of a little forethought, that I let out what passed in my mind with too little ceremony for making up again. However, I gave her the baubles; which she accepted out of hand; and made free to ask me to add something more, to make her amends for waiting for nothing; which was but fair; though it showed me that when she had lost her pretty face, she had no great matter to boast of in point of a noble way of thinking. I hope, else, I should have been above playing her false; without which I should be little to chose from a scoundrel. But she was in such a main hurry to secure herself the rhino, that it's my brief that her inside, if I could have got a look at it, was but little short, in point of ugliness, to her outside. Howbeit, I used her handsomely, and we parted friends.'

The Admiral here walked about the room, a little disturbed, and then continued his narrative.

He crossed the Straits, having always preserved the direction of the lady of the castle near the convent; but the Revolution was then flaming; the castle had been burnt; all the family was dispersed; and he was warned not to make any enquiry even after the parson. But he grew sick of the whole business, and not sorry to cut it short, upon hearing that his niece, who was known by the appellation of Mademoiselle Juliette, was married to a French monsieur. He was coming away, in deep disgust, and burning wrath, when he was seized himself, and put into prison by order of Mr Robespierre. But this durance did not last long; for he joined a party that was just getting off, and returned to Great Britain; and moreover, though little enough to his knowledge, in the very same vessel that brought over his niece. 'And here, my dear girl, is the finish of all I have to recount. But what I observe, with no great pleasure, if I should tell you my remark, is, that, while, for so many years, I have given up my head to nothing but thinking of my niece,—to the exception of poor Jenny

Barker,—she does not seem so much as ever to have heard, or thought about her uncle?'

Juliet assured him, on the contrary, that her grandmother Powel had talked unceasingly of her son; but that, tender-hearted, timid, and devoted to Lord Granville, she had never ventured to trust to a letter a secret that demanded so much discretion; and had therefore postponed all communication to their meeting; of which she had lived in the constant hope. And Juliet herself, since the afflicting loss of that excellent lady, always believing him to be in the East Indies, had never dared claim his parentage, nor solicit his favour; her peculiar and unhappy situation making all written accounts, not only of her affairs, but of her name and her residence, dangerous.

This brought the conversation back to herself. ''Tis remarkable enough,' said the Admiral, 'that, in all this long parley, we have not yet said an item about the worst part of the job,—your marriage! How came you here without your husband? For all I have no great goust to your marrying in that sort, God forbid I should uphold a wife in running away from her lawful spouse, even though he be a Frenchman! We should always do right, for the sake of shaming wrong. A man, being the higher vessel, may marry all over the globe, and take his wife to his home; but a woman, as she is only given him for his help-mate, must tack about after him, and come to the same anchorage.'

Sadness now clouded the skin, and dimmed the eyes of Juliet. The story which she had to reveal, the hard necessity of separating herself from so near a relation, and so kind a protector, at the very moment of an apparent union; joined to the obstacles which his prejudices and feelings might put in the way of her decided sacrifice; made the avowal of her intention seem almost as difficult as its execution.

'Don't be cast down, however, my girl,' continued the Admiral; 'for when things are come to the worst, as I have taken frequent note, they often veer about, nobody knows how, and turn out for the best. I should as lieve you had not tied such an ugly knot, I won't say to the contrary; howbeit, as the thing is done, we may as well make the best of it. The man may be a tolerable good Christian, mayhap, for a Papist. And indeed, to tell you the truth, though it is a thing I am not over fond of speaking about, I have seen some Frenchmen I could have liked mightily myself, if I had not known where they came from. I had some prisoners once aboard, that were as likely men, and as much of gentlemen, and as agreeable behaved, and had as good sense, too, of their own, as if they had been Englishmen. Perhaps your husband may be one of them? If so, let him come over here, and he shall want for nothing. I am always proud to shew old England; so invite him, my dear, to come.'

'Alas!—alas!—'cried Juliet, weeping.

'What! he is but a sorry dog, then? Well, I can't pretend to be surprized at that. However, I'll tie up your fortune, and won't let him touch a penny of it, but upon condition that you come over for it yourself once a year. And now I have you safe and sure, I shall carry my codicil to Lord Denmeath,—a fellow of steel, they say!—and get you your thirty thousand pounds; for that, I am told, is the portion of the lady of quality's daughter. But all I shall give you myself shall only be bit by bit, till I know how that sorry fellow uses you. It's a main pity you threw yourself away in such a hurry! But I suppose he's a fine likely young dog?

'Hideous! hideous!' off all guard, exclaimed the shuddering Juliet.

'Why, then, most like, you only married him for the sake of a little palaver? Poor girl! However, it's done, and a husband's a husband; so I'll ask no more questions.'

Kissing her then very kindly, he said he would go and suck in a little fresh breeze upon the beech, to calm his spirits; for he felt as if he had been steering his vessel in a hurricane.

He asked her to accompany him; but she desired a little stillness and rest. He shook hands with her, and, with a look of concern, said, 'My sister did but a foolish thing, after all, in marrying that young lord, however the world may judge it to have been an ambitious one. You would never have been smuggled out of your native land, in that fashion, if she had taken up with a man in her own rank of life: some honest tar, for example! for, to my seeming, there is not an honester person in the whole world, nor a person of more honour, than a British tar! And yet,—see the difference of those topsy-turvy marriages!—a worthy tar would have been proud of my sister for his wife; while your lord was only ashamed of her! for that's the bottom of the story, put what dust you will in your eyes for the top!'

CHAPTER XCI

Juliet, left alone, again vented her full heart by tears. Happiness never seemed within her reach, but to make her feel more severely the hard necessity that it must be resigned. All her tenderest affections had been delighted, and her most ardent wishes surpassed, in being recognized as his niece by a man of so much worth, honour, and benevolence as the Admiral; and her heart had been yet more exquisitely touched, by acknowledged affinity with so sweet a character as that of Lady Aurora; her portion, by the duplicate-codicil, flattered, and gave dignity to her softest feelings;—nevertheless, the cruelty of her situation was in nothing altered; the danger of the Bishop was still the same; the same, therefore, was her duty. Even for deliberation she allowed herself no choice, save whether to confess to the Admiral the dreadful nature of her call to the Continent; or to go thither simply as a thing of course, to join her husband.

For the latter, his approvance was declared; for the former, even his consent might be withdrawn: to spare, therefore, to his kind heart the unavailing knowledge of her misery; and to herself the useless conflicts that might ensue from the discovery; she ultimately decided to set out upon her voyage, with her story and misfortunes unrevealed.

This plan determined upon, she struggled to fortify her mind for its execution, by endeavouring to consider as her husband the man to whom, in any manner, she had given her hand; since so, only, she could seek to check the disgust with which she shrunk from him as her deadliest foe. She remembered, and even sought to call back, the terrific scruples with which she had been seized, when, while striving to escape, she heard him assert that she was his wife, and felt powerless to disvow his claim. Triumphant, menacing, and ferocious, she had fled him without hesitation, though not completely without doubt; but when she beheld him seized, in custody,—and heard him call her husband! and saw herself considered as his wife! duty, for that horrible instant, seemed in his favour; and, had not Sir Jaspar summoned her by her maiden name, to attend her own nearest relations, all her resistance had been subdued, by an overwhelming dread that to resist might possibly be wrong.

Recollection, also, told her that, at the epoch when, with whatever misery, she had suffered him to take her hand, no mental reservation had prepared for future flight and disavowal: she laboured therefore, now, to plead to herself the vows which she had listened to, though she had not pronounced; and to animate her sacrifice by the terrour of perjury.

Nevertheless, all these virtuous arguments against her own freedom, were insufficient to convince her that her marriage was valid. The violent constraint, the forced rites, the interrupted ceremony, the omission of every religious form;—no priest, no church to sanctify even appearances;—No! she cried, no! I am not his wife! even were it my wish, even were he all I prize upon earth, still I should fly him till we were joined by holier bands! Nevertheless, for the Bishop I meant the sacrifice, and, since so, only, he can be preserved;—for the Bishop I must myself invite its more solemn ratification!

Satisfied that this line of conduct, while dictated by tender gratitude, was confirmed by severer justice; she would not trust herself again with the sight of Lady Aurora, till measures were irreversibly taken for her departure; and, upon the return of the Admiral from his walk, she communicated to him, though without any explanation, her urgent desire to make the voyage with all possible expedition.

The Admiral, persuaded that her haste was to soften the harsh treatment of a husband who had inveigled her into marriage by flattery and falsehood, forbore either questions or comments; though he looked at her with commiseration; often shaking his head, with an expression that implied: What pity to have thrown yourself thus away! His high notions, nevertheless, of conjugal prerogative, made him approve and second her design; and, saying that he saw nothing gained by delay, but breeding more bad blood, he told her that he would conduct her to —— himself, the next morning; and stay with her till he could procure her a proper passage; engaging to present her wherewithal to ascertain for her a good and hearty reception; with an assurance to her husband, that she should, at any time, have the same sum, only for fetching it in person.

This promising opening to occasional re-unions, gave her, now, more fortitude for announcing to her gentle sister the fixed approaching separation. But, though these were softening circumstances to their parting, Lady Aurora heard the decision with despair; and though the discovery of an uncle, a protector, in so excellent a man as the Admiral, offered a prospect of solid comfort; still she could dwell only upon the forced ties, the unnatural connexion, and the brutal character to which her unhappy sister must be the victim.

Each seeking, nevertheless, to console the other, though each, herself, was inconsolable, they passed together the rest of the melancholy, yet precious day; uninterrupted by the Admiral; who was engaged to dine out in the neighbourhood; or even by Mrs Howel; who acquiesced, perforce, to the pleadings of Lady Aurora; in suffering her ladyship to remain in her own room with Juliet.

They engaged to meet again by daybreak, the next morning, though to meet but to part. The next morning, however, when summoned to a post-chaise by the Admiral, the courage of Juliet, for so dreadful a leave-taking, failed; and, committing to paper a few piercingly tender words, she determined to write, more at length, all the consolation that she could suggest from the first stage.

But when, in speechless grief, she would have felt her little billet in the anti-room, she found Lady Aurora's woman already in attendance; and heard that Lady Aurora, also, was risen and dressed. She feared, therefore, now, that an evasion might rather aggravate than spare affliction to her beloved sister; and, repressing her own feelings, entered the chamber.

Lady Aurora, who had scarcely closed her eyes all night, had now, in the fancied security of a meeting, from having placed her maid as a sentinel, just dropt asleep. Her pale cheeks, and the movement of sorrow still quivering upon her lips, shewed that she had been weeping, when overpowering fatigue had induced a short slumber. Juliet, in looking at her, thought she contemplated an angel. The touching innocence of her countenance; the sweetness which no sadness could destroy; the grief exempt from impatience; and the air of purity that overspread her whole face, and seemed breathing round her whole form, inspired Juliet, for a few moments, with ideas too sublime for mere sublunary sorrow. She knelt, with tender reverence, by her side, inwardly ejaculating, Sleep on, my angel sister! Recruit your harassed spirits, and wake not yet to the woes of your hapless Juliet! Then, placing gently upon her bosom the written farewell, she softly kissed the hem of her garments, and glided from the room.

She made a sign to the maid, for she had no power of utterance, not to awaken her lady; and hurried down stairs to join the Admiral, attended by the faithful Ambroise.

She was spared offering any apologies for detaining her uncle, by finding him preparing to step down to the beach, with a spying glass, without which he never stirred a step; to take a view, before they set off, of a sail, which his servant, an old seaman, had just brought him word was in sight. He helped her, therefore, into the chaise, begging her patience for a few minutes.

Juliet was not sorry to seize this interval for returning to the anti-room, to learn whether Lady Aurora were awake; and, by her resignation or emotion, to judge whether a parting embrace would prove baneful or soothing.

As she was re-entering the house, a vociferous cry of 'Stop! stop!' issued from a carriage that was driving past. She went on, desiring Ambroise to give her notice when the Admiral came back; but had not yet reached the gallery, when the stairs were rapidly ascended by two, or more persons, one of which encircled her in his arms.

She shrieked with sudden horrour and despair, strenuously striving to disengage herself; though persuaded that the only person who would dare thus to assail her, was him to whom she was intentionally resigning her destiny; but her instinctive resistance was short; a voice that spoke love and sweetness exclaimed. 'Miss Ellis! sweet, lovely Miss Ellis! you are, then, my sister!'

'Ah heavens! kind heaven!' cried the delighted Juliet, 'is it you, Lord Melbury? and do you,—will you,—and thus kindly, own me?'

'Own? I am proud of you! My other sister alone can be as dear to me! what two incomparable creatures has heaven bestowed upon me for my sisters! How hard I must work not to disgrace them! And I will work hard, too! I will not see two such treasures, so near to me, and so dear to me, hold down their sweet heads with shame for their brother. Come with me, then, my new sister! —you need not fear to trust yourself with me now! Come, for I have something to say that we must talk over together alone.'

Putting, then, her willing arm within his, he eagerly conducted her down stairs; made her pass by the astonished Ambroise, at whom she nodded and smiled in the fulness of her contentment, and led her towards the beach; her heart exulting, and her eyes glistening with tender joy; even while every nerve was affected, and all her feelings were tortured, by a dread of quick approaching separation and misery.

'I am come,' cried he, when they were at a little distance from the houses, 'to take the most prompt advantage of my brotherly character. I have travelled all night, not to lose a moment in laying my scheme before you.'

'What kindness!—Oh my lord!—and where did you hear,—where did Sir Jaspar's letter reach you?'

'Sir Jaspar?—I have received no letter from Sir Jaspar. I have seen no Sir Jaspar!'

'How, then, is it possible you can know—'

'Oh ho! you think you have no friend, then, but Sir Jaspar? And you suppose, perhaps, that you have no admirer but Sir Jaspar?'

'I am sure, at least, there is no other person to whom I have revealed my name.'

'Then he must have betrayed it to some other himself, my sweet sister! for 'tis not from him I have had my intelligence. Be less sure, therefore, for the future, of an old man, and trust a younger one more willingly! However, there is no time now for raillery; a messenger is waiting the result of our conference. I am fully informed, my precious sister, of your terrible situation; I will not stop now to execrate your infernal pursuer, though he will not lose my execrations by the delay! I know, too, your sublime resolution to save our dear guardian,—for yours is ours!—that good and reverend Bishop; and to look upon yourself to be tied up, as a bond-woman, till you are formally released form those foul shackles. Do I state the case right?'

'Oh far, far too acurately! And even now, at a moment so blest! I must tear myself away,—by my own will, with whatever horrour!—from the sweetest of sisters,—from you, my kindest brother!—and from the most benevolent of uncles, by a separation a thousand times more dreadful than any death!'

'Take comfort, sweet sister! take comfort, loveliest Miss Ellis!—for I can't help calling you Miss Ellis, now and then, a little while longer:—I have a plan to make you free! to set you completely at liberty, and yet save that excellent Bishop!—'

'Oh my lord! how heavenly an idea!—but how impossible!'

'Not at all! 'tis the easiest thing in the world! only hear me. That wretch who claims you, shall have the portion he demands; the six thousand pounds; immediately upon signing your release, sending over the promissory-note of Lord Denmeath, and delivering your noble Bishop into the hands of the person who shall carry over the money; which, however, shall only be paid at some frontier town, whence the Bishop may come instantly hither.'

Struck with rapturous surprize, Juliet scarcely restrained herself form falling at his feet. She pressed his arm, she kissed the edge of his coat, and, while striving, inarticulately, to call for blessings upon his head, burst into a passion of tears,—though tears of ecstatic joy,—that nearly deprived her of respiration.

'My sister! my dear sister!' tenderly cried Lord Melbury, 'how ashamed you make me! Could you, then, expect less? What a poor opinion you have entertained of your poor brother! I give you nothing! I merely agree that you shall possess what is your due. Know you not that you are entitled to thirty thousand pounds from our estate? To the same fortune that has been settled upon Aurora? 'Tis from your own portion, only, my poor sister, that this six thousand will be sunk.'

'Can you, then, generous, generous Lord Melbury!—can you see thus, without regret, without murmur, so capital a sum suddenly and unexpectedly torn from you?'

'I have not yet enjoyed it, my dear sister; I shall not, therefore, miss it. But if I had possessed it always, should I not be paid, ten million of times paid, by finding such a new sister? I shall be proud to shew the whole world I know how to prize such a relation. And I will not have them think me such a mere boy, because I am still rather young, as to be at a loss how to act by myself. I shall not, therefore, consult my uncle, for I am determined not to be ruled by him. I will solemnly bind myself to pay your whole fortune the moment I am of age. It is my duty, and my pride, and, at the same time, my delight, to spare your delicacy, as well as my own character, and our dear father's memory, any process, or any dispute.'

Then, opening his arms, with design to embrace her, but checking himself upon recollecting that he might be observed, he animatedly added, 'Yes, my dear father! I will shew how I cherish your memory, by my care of your eldest born! by my care of her interests, her safety, and her happiness!—As to her honour,' he added, with a conscious smile, 'she has shewn me that she knows how to be its guardian herself!'

The grateful Juliet frankly acknowledged, that both the thought and the wish had frequently occurred to her, of rescuing the Bishop, through her portion, without herself: but she had been utterly powerless to raise it. She was under age, and uncertain whether her rights might ever be proved: and the six thousand pounds proffered by Lord Denmeath, she was well aware, would never be accorded but to establish her as an alien. Her generous brother, by anticipating, as well as confirming her claims, alone could realize such a project. With sensations, then, of unmixed felicity, that seemed lifting her, while yet on earth, into heaven, she was flying to call for the participation of Lady Aurora, and of her uncle, in her joy; when Lord Melbury, stopping her, said, that all was not yet prepared for communication.

'You clearly,' he continued, 'agree to the scheme?'

'With transport!' she cried; 'and with eternal thankfulness!'

Without delay, then, he said, they must appoint a person of trust, who knew the French language well, and to whom the whole history might be confided; to carry over the offer, and the money, and to bring back the Bishop.

'And I have a friend,' he continued, 'now ready for the enterprize. One equally able and willing to claim the Bishop, and to give undoubted security for the six thousand pounds. Can you form any notion who such a man may be?'

He looked at her gaily, yet with a scrutiny that made her blush. One person only could occur to her; but occurred with an alarming sense of impropriety in allowing him such an employment, that instantly damped her high delight. She dropt her eyes; an unrepressed sigh broke from her heart; but secret consciousness hushed all enquiry into the truth of her conjecture.

In silence, too, for a moment, Lord Melbury contemplated her; struck with her sudden sadness, and uncertain to what it might be attributed. Affectionately, then, taking her hand, 'I must come,' he cried, 'to the point, or my messenger will lose his patience. Proposals of marriage the most honourable have been made to me; such, my dear sister, as merit my best interest with you. The person is unexceptionable, high in mind, manners, and family, and has long been attached to you—'

Juliet here, with dignity, interrupted him, 'My lord, I will not ask who this may be; I even beg not to be told. I can listen to no one! Till the Bishop is released and safe, I hold myself merely to be his hostage; and, till my freedom, atrociously as it has been violated, shall be legally restored to me, I cannot but feel hurt,—for I will not say offended where the intention is so kind, and so pure,—that any proposals of any sort, and from any person, should be addressed to me!'

Lord Melbury, prepared for expostulation, was beginning to reply; but she solemnly besought him not to involve her in any new conflicts.

She then asked his permission to introduce him to her uncle, Admiral Powel; whom she desired to join upon the beach.

No, no; he answered; other business, still more urgent, must have precedence. And, holding both her hands, he insisted upon acquainting, her, that it was Mr Harleigh who had been his informant of her history and situation; and that she was the undoubted and legitimate daughter of Lord Granville; all which he had learnt from Sir Jaspar Herrington. 'And Mr Harleigh has begged my leave,' continued his lordship, smiling, 'though I am not, you may think, perhaps, very old for judging of such matters; to make his addresses to you.— Now don't put yourself into that flutter till you hear how he arranged it; for he knows all your scruples, and reveres them,—or, rather, and reveres you, my sweet sister! for your scruples we both think a little chimerical: don't be angry at that; we honour you all the same for having them: and Mr Harleigh seems to adore you only the more. So, I make no doubt does Aurora. And I, too, my dear sister! only I can't see you sacrificed to them. But Mr Harleigh has found a way to reconcile all perplexities. He will save you, he says, in honour as well as in person; for the wretch shall still have the wife whom he married, if he will restore the Bishop!'

'What can you mean?'—

'His six thousand pounds, my dear sister! That sum, in full, he shall have; for that, as Harleigh says, is the wife that he married!'

Smiles now again, irresistibly, forced their way back to the face of Juliet, as she bowed her full concurrence to this observation.

'Harleigh, therefore,' continued Lord Melbury, 'for this very reason, will go himself to make the arrangement; to the end that, if the wretch refuses to take the six thousand without you, he may offer a thousand, or two, over: for, enraged as he is to enrich such a scoundrel, he would rather endow him with your whole thirty thousand, and, for aught I know, with as much more of his own, than let you fall into his clutches.'

The eyes of Juliet again swam in tears. 'Noble, incomparable Harleigh!' she irresistibly ejaculated; but, checking herself, 'My lord,' she said, 'my thanks are still all that I can return to Mr Harleigh,—yet I will not deny how much I am touched by his generosity. But I have insurmountable objections to this proposition; now, indeed, ought I to cast upon any other, the risks of an engagement which honour and conscience make sacred to myself.'

'Poor Harleigh!' said Lord Melbury, 'I have been but a bad advocate, he will think! You will at least see him?'

'See him?'

'Yes; he came with me hither. 'Twas he descried you first, as you got out of the post-chaise. He was accompanying me up the stairs: but he retreated. You will surely see him?'

'No, my Lord, no!—certainly not!'

'What! not for a moment? Oh, that would be too barbarous!'

With these words, he ran back to the town.

Juliet called after him; but in vain.

Her heart now beat high; it seemed throbbing through her bosom; but she bent her way towards the beach, to secure her safety by joining her uncle.

She perceived him at some distance, in the midst of a small group; conspicuous from his height, his naval air and equipment, and his long spying glass; which he occasionally brandished, as he seemed questioning, or haranguing the people around him.

In a minute, she was accosted by the old sailor, who was sent by his master to the chaise, in which he supposed his niece to be still waiting; to beg that she would not be impatient, because a boat being just come in, with a small handful of the enemy, his honour was giving a look at the vessel, to see to its being wind and weather proof, to the end that her ladyship might take a sail in it.

Juliet, though she answered, 'Certainly; tell my uncle certainly;' knew not what she heard, nor what she said; confused by fast approaching footsteps, which told her that she could not, now, either by going on or by turning back, escape meeting Harleigh.

Lord Melbury advanced first; and, willing to give Harleigh a moment to press his suit, good humouredly addressed the sailor, with enquiries of what was going forward upon the beach. Harleigh, having made a bow, which her averted eyes had not seen, drew back, distressed and irresolute, waiting to catch a look that might be his guide. But when, from the discourse of the sailor with Lord Melbury, he learnt the arrival of a small vessel form the Continent, which was destined immediately to return thither; he precipitately took his lordship by the arm, spoke to him a few words apart, and then flew forward to the strand.

Juliet, disturbed by new fears, permitted her countenance to make enquiries which her tongue durst not pronounce; and Lord Melbury, who understood her, frankly said, 'He is a man, sister, of ten thousand! He will sail a race with you, and strive which shall get in first to save the Bishop!'

Juliet felt thunderstruck; Harleigh seeking a passage in the very vessel which seemed pitched upon by her uncle for her own voyage! That they should go together was not to be thought of; but to suffer him to risk becoming the victim to her promise and her duties, was grief and shame and terrour united! Her eyes affrightedly pursued him, till he entered into the group upon the strand; and her perturbation then was so extreme, that she felt inclined to forfeit, by one dauntless stroke, the delicacy which, as yet, had through life, been the prominent feature of her character, by darting on, openly to conjure him to return. But habits which have been formed upon principle, and embellished by self-approbation, withstand, upon the smallest reflection, every wish, and every feeling that would excite their violation. The idea, therefore, died in its birth; and she sought to compose her disordered spirits, by silent prayers for courage and resignation.

With the most fraternal participation in her palpable distress, Lord Melbury endeavoured to offer her consolation; till the sailor, who had returned to the Admiral, came from him, a second time, to desire that she would hasten upon the beach, 'to help his honour, please your ladyship,' said the merry tar, with a significant nod, 'to a little French lingo; these mounseers and their wives,—if, behaps, they be'n't only their sweethearts; not over and above understanding his honour.'

Juliet moved slowly on: the Admiral, used to more prompt obedience, came forward to hasten her, calling out, as soon as she was within hearing, 'Please to wag a little nimbler, niece; for here are some outlandish gentry come over, that speak so fast, one after t'other; or else all at a time; each telling his own story; or, for aught I can make out, each telling the same thing one as t'other; that, though I try my best to understand them, not being willing to dash them, I can't make out above one word in a dozen, if you take it upon an average, of what they say. However, though it is our duty to hold them all as our native enemies; and I shall never, God willing, see them in any other light; yet it would be but unchristian not to lend them an hand, when they are chopfallen and sorrowful; and, moreover, consumedly out of cash. So if I can help them, I see no reason to the contrary; for my enemy in distress is my friend: because why? I was only his enemy to get the upper hand of him.'

Then, turning to Lord Melbury and Harleigh, 'I hope,' he added, 'you won't think me wanting to my country, if, for the honour of old England, I give these poor half-starved souls a hearty meal of good roast beef, with a bumper of Dorchester ale, and Devonshire cyder? things which I conclude they have never yet tasted from their births to this hour; their own washy diet of soup meagre and sallad, with which I would not fatten a sparrow, being what they are more naturally born to. And I sha'n't be sorry, I confess, to shew the French we have a little politeness of our own; which, by what I have often taken note, I rather surmize they hold to be a merchandize of their own monopoly. And so, if you all think well of it, we'll tack about, and give them an handsome invitation out of hand; for when a person stops to ponder before he does a good office, 'tis a sign he had full as lieve let it alone.'

Juliet readily complied, though she could not readily speak; but what was her perturbation, the next moment, to see Harleigh vehemently break from the group by which he had been surrounded, rush precipitately forward to meet them, and, singling out Lord Melbury encircle his lordship in his arms, exclaiming, 'My lord! my dear lord! your sister is free!—I claim, now, your suffrage!—Her brutal persecutor, convicted of heading a treasonable conspiracy in his own country, has paid the forfeit of his crimes! These passengers bring the tidings! My lord! my dear lord! your sister is free!'—

Juliet, who heard, as it was meant that she should hear, this passionate address, felt suspended in all her faculties. Joy, in the first instant, sought precedence; but it was supplanted, in another moment, by tearful incredulity; and she stood motionless, speechless, scarcely conscious whether she were alive.

An exclamation of 'What's all this?' from the astonished Admiral; and a juvenile jump of unrestrained rapture from the transported Lord Melbury, brought Harleigh to himself. He felt confounded at the publicity and the abruptness of an address into which his ecstacy had surprized him; yet his satisfaction was too high for repentance, though he forced it to submit to some controul.

Suspension of sensibility could not, while there was life, be long allowed to Juliet; and the violence of her emotions, at its return, almost burst her bosom. What a change! her feet tottered; she sustained her shaking frame against the Admiral; she believed herself in some new existence! yet it was not unmixed joy that she experienced; there was something in the nature of her deliverance repulsive to joy; and the perturbed and tumultuous sensations which rushed into her breast, seemed overpowering her strength, and almost shattering even her comprehension; till she was brought back painfully to herself, by an abrupt recollection of the uncertainty of the fate of the Bishop; and, shudderingly, she exclaimed, 'Oh if my revered guardian be not safe!'—

The wondering Admiral now, addressing Harleigh, gravely begged to be made acquainted, in plainer words, with the news that he reported.

Not sorry to repeat what he wished should be fully comprehended, Harleigh, more composedly, recounted his intelligence; dwelling upon details which brought conviction of the seizure, the trial, and the execution of the execrable commissary.

Juliet listened with rapt attention; but in proportion as her security in her own safety became confirmed, her poignant solicitude for that of the Bishop increased; and again she exclaimed, 'Oh! if my guardian has not escaped!'

The Admiral, turning towards her rather austerely, said, 'You must have had but a sad dog of a husband, Niece Granville, to think only of an old priest, when you hear of his demise! However, to my seeming, though he might be but a rogue, a husband's a husband; and I don't much uphold a wife's not thinking of that; for, if a woman may mutiny against her husband, there's an end of all discipline.'

Overwhelmed with shame, Juliet could attempt no self defence; but Lord Melbury warmly assured the Admiral, that his niece, Miss Granville, had never really been married; that a forced, interrupted, and unfinished lay-ceremony, had mockingly been celebrated; accompanied by circumstances atrocious, infamous, and cruel: and that the marriage could never have been valid, either in sight of the church, or of her own conscience.

The Admiral, with avidity and rising delight, sucked in this vindication; and then whispered to Juliet, 'Pray, if I may make so free, who is this pretty boy, that's got so much more insight into your affairs than I have? He's a very pretty boy; but I have no great taste to being put in the rear by him!'

Juliet was beginning to reply, when the Admiral called out, in a tone of some chagrin, 'Now we are put off from doing the handsome thing! for here's the outlandish gentry coming among us before we have invited them! And now, you'll see, they'll always stand to it that they have the upper hand of us English in politeness! And I had rather have seen them all at the devil!'

Juliet, looking forward, perceived that they were approached by some strangers of a foreign appearance; but they detained not her attention; at one side, and somewhat aloof from them, a form caught her eye, reverend, aged, infirm. She started, and with almost agonized earnestness, advanced rapidly a few steps; then stopt abruptly to renew her examination; but presently, advancing again, called out, 'Merciful Heaven!' and, rushing on, with extended arms, and uncontrolled rapture, threw herself at the feet of the ancient traveller; and, embracing his knees, sobbed rather than articulated, in French, 'My guardian! my preserver! my more than father!—I have not then lost you!'

Deeply affected, the man of years bent over, and blessed her; mildly, yet fondly, uttering, in the same language, 'My child! my Juliet!—Do I then behold you again, my excellent child!'

Then, helping her to rise, he added, 'Your willing martyrdom is spared, my dear, my adopted daughter! and I, most mercifully! am spared its bitter infliction. Thanksgiving are all we have to offer, thanksgiving and humble prayers for UNIVERSAL PEACE!'

With anxious tenderness Juliet enquired for her benefactress, the Marchioness; and the Bishop for his niece Gabriella. The Marchioness was safe and well, awaiting a general re-union with her family; Gabriella, therefore, Juliet assured the Bishop, was now, probably in her revered mother's arms.

All further detail, whether of her own difficulties and sufferings, or of the perils and escapes of the Bishop, during their long separation, they mutually set apart for future communication; every evil, for the present, being sunk in gratitude at their meeting.

Harleigh, who witnessed this scene with looks of love and joy, though not wholly unmixed with suffering impatience, forced himself to stand aloof. Lord Melbury, who had no feeling to hide, nor result to fear, gaily capered with unrestrained delight; and the Admiral, impressed with wonder, yet reverence, his hat in his hand, and his head high up in the air, waited patiently for a pause; and then, bowing to the ground, solemnly said, 'Mr Bishop, you are welcome to old England! heartily welcome, Mr Bishop! I ought to beg your pardon, perhaps, for speaking to you in English; but I have partly forgot my French; which, not to mince the matter, I never thought it much worth while to study; little enough devizing I should ever meet with a native-born Frenchman who was so honest a man! For it's pretty much our creed, aboard, though I don't over and above uphold it myself, except as far as may belong to the sea-service,—to look upon your nation as little better than a cluster of rogues. However, we of the upper class, knowing that we are all alike, in the main, of God's workmanship, don't account it our duty to hold you so cheap. Therefore, Mr Bishop, you are heartily welcome to old England.'

The Bishop smiled; too wise to be offended, where he saw that no offence was meant.

'But, for all that,' the Admiral continued, 'I can't deny but I had as lieve, to the full, if I had had my choice, that my niece should not have been brought up by the enemy; yet I have always had a proper respect for a parson, whether he be of the true religion, or only a Papist. I hold nothing narrower than despising a man for his ignorance; especially when it's only of the apparatus, and not of the solid part. My niece, Mr Bishop, will tell you the heads of what I say in your own proper dialect.'

The Bishop answered, that he perfectly understood English.

'I am cordially glad to hear it!' cried the Admiral, holding out his hand to him; 'for that's an item that gives; me at once a good opinion of you! A man can be no common person who has a taste for our sterling sense, after being brought up to frothy compliments; and therefore, Mr Bishop, I beg you to favour me with your company to eat a bit of roast beef with us at our lodging-house; after our plain old English fashion: which, if I should make free to tell you what passes in my mind, I hold to be far wholesomer than your ragouts and fricandos, made up of oil and grease. But I only drop that as a matter of opinion; every nation having a right to like best what it can get cheapest. And if the rest of the passengers are people of a right way of thinking, I beg you to tell them I shall be glad of the favour of their company too.'

The Bishop bowed, with an air of mild satisfaction.

'And I heartily wish you would give me an item, Monsieur the Bishop, how I might behave more handsomely; for, by what I can make out, you have been as kind to my niece, as if you had been born on this side the Channel; which is no small compliment to make to one born on t'other side; and if ever I forget it, I wish I may go to the bottom! a thing we seamen, who understand something of those matters, (smiling,) had full as lief leave alone.'

He then recommended to them all to stroll upon the sands for a further whet to their appetite; while he went himself to the lodging-house, to see what could be had for a repast.

CHAPTER XCII

Happy to second the benevolent scheme of the kind-hearted Admiral, the Bishop hastened to his fellow-voyagers with the hospitable invitation. Juliet, in whom every feeling was awake to meet, to embrace, and to share her delight with Lady Aurora, would have followed; but Lord Melbury, to avoid, upon so interesting an occasion, any interruption from Mrs Howel, objected to returning to the hotel; and proposed being the messenger to fetch their sister. Juliet joyfully consented, and went to await them in the beautiful verdant recess, between two rocks, overlooking the vast ocean, with which she had already been so much charmed.

No sooner, at this favourite spot, was Juliet alone, than, according to her wonted custom, she vented the fulness of her heart in pious acknowledgements. She had scarcely risen, when again,—though without Lady Aurora,—she saw Lord Melbury; yet not alone; he was arm in arm with Harleigh. 'My dear new sister,' he gaily cried, 'I go now for Aurora. We shall be here presently; but Mr Harleigh is so kind as to promise that he will stand without, as sentinel, to see that no one approaches nor disturbs you.'

He was gone while yet speaking.

The immediate impulse of Juliet urged her to remonstrance, or flight; but it was the impulse of habit, not of reason; an instant, and a look of Harleigh, represented that the total change of her situation, authorized, on all sides, a total change of conduct.

Every part of her frame partook of the emotion with which this sudden consciousness beat at her heart; while her silence, her unresisting stay, and the sight of her varying complexion, thrilled to the soul of Harleigh, with an encouragement that he trembled with impatience to exchange for certainty. 'At last,—at last,—may I,' he cried, 'under the sanction of a brother, presume upon obtaining a hearing with some little remittance of reserve? of mistrust?'

Juliet dropt her head.

'Will not Miss Granville be more gracious than Miss Ellis has been? Miss Granville can have no tie but what is voluntary: no hovering doubts, no chilling scruples, no fancied engagements—'

A half sigh, of too recent recollection, heaved the breast of Juliet.

'To plead,' he continued, 'against all confidence; to freeze every avenue to sympathy; to repel, or wound every rising hope! Miss Granville, is wholly independent; mistress of her heart, mistress of herself—'

'No, Mr Harleigh, no!' with quickness, though with gentleness, interrupted Juliet.

Harleigh, momentarily startled, ventured to bend his head below her bonnet; and saw, then, that the blush which had visited, flown, and re-visited her face, had fixed itself in the deepest tint upon her cheek. He gazed upon her in ecstatic silence, till, looking up, and, for the first time, suffering her eyes willingly to meet his, 'No, Mr Harleigh, no!' she softly repeated, 'I am not so independent!' A smile then beamed over her features, so radiant, so embellishing, that Harleigh wondered he had ever thought her beautiful before, as she added, 'Had I an hundred hearts,—ten thousand times you must have conquered them all!'

Rapture itself, now, is too cold a word,—or too common a one,—to give an adequate idea of the bliss of Harleigh. He took her no longer reluctant hand, and she felt upon it a burning tear as he pressed it to his lips; but his joy was unutterable. The change was so great, so sudden, and so exquisite, from all he most dreaded to all he most desired, that language seemed futile for its expression: and to look at her without fearing to alarm or offend her; to meet, with the softest assurance of partial favour, those eyes hitherto so coldly averted; to hold, unresisted, the fair hand that, but the moment before, it seemed sacrilege even to wish to touch; so, only, could he demonstrate the fulness of his transport, the fervour of his gratitude, the perfection of his felicity.

In Juliet, though happiness was not less exalted, pleasure wore the chastened garb of moderation, even in the midst of a frankness that laid open her heart. Yet, seeing his suit thus authorized by her brother, and certain of the approbation of the Bishop, and of her uncle, to so equal and honourable an alliance; she indulged her soft propensities in his favour, by gently conceding avowals, that rewarded not alone his persevering constancy, but her own long and difficult forbearance. 'Many efforts, many conflicts,' she cried, 'in my cruel trials, I have certainly found harder; but none, none so distasteful, as the unremitting necessity of seeming always impenetrable—where most I was sensitive!'

'By sweetness such as this,' cried Harleigh, 'you would almost persuade me to rejoice at a suspense that has nearly maddened me! Yet,—could you have conceived the agony, the despair of my mind, at your icy, relentless silence! not once to trust me as a friend! not one moment to confide in my integrity! never to consult, to commune, to speak, nor to hear!—You smile?—Can it be at the pain you have inflicted?'—

'Oh no, no, no! If I smile, 'tis at the greater pain I have, I trust, averted! While conscious that I might, eventually, be chained to another, every duty admonished me to resist every feeling!—Yet with hope always, ultimately, before me, I had not the force to utter a word,—a baneful word!—that might teach you to renounce me!—even though I deemed it indispensable to my honour to exact a total separation. Had I confided to you my fearful secret,— had you yourself aided the abolition of my shackles, should I not, in a situation so delicate, so critical, have fixed an eternal barrier between us,—or have sacrificed the fame of both to the most wounding of calumnies? Ah no! from the instant that my heart interfered,—that I was conscious of a new motive that urged my wish of liberation,—I have held it my duty, I have felt it my future happiness, to avoid,—to fear,—to fly you!—'

'I was most favoured, then, it seems,' replied Harleigh, with a smile of rapture, 'when I thought you most inexorable? I must thank you for your rejections, your avoidance, your implacable, immoveable coldness?'

'Reverse, else, the medal,' cried she, gaily, 'and see whether the impression will be more to your taste!'

'Loveliest Miss Ellis! most beloved Miss Granville! My own,—at length! at length! my own sweet Juliet! that, and that only can be to my taste which has brought me to the bliss of this moment!'

With blushing tenderness, Juliet then confessed, that at the moment of his first generous declaration, following the summer-house scene with Elinor, she had felt pierced with an aggravated horrour of her nameless ties, that had nearly burst her heart asunder.

With minute retrospection, then, enjoying even every evil, and finding motives of congratulation from every pain that was past, they mutually recapitulated their feelings, their conjectures, their rising and progressive partiality, since the opening of their acquaintance. One circumstance alone was tinted with regret,—'Elinor?' cried Juliet, 'Oh! how will Elinor bear to hear of this event!'

'Fear her not!' he returned. 'She has a noble, though, perhaps, a masculine spirit, and she will soon, probably, think of this affair only with pique and wonder,—not against me, for she is truly generous; but against herself, for she is candid and just. She has always internally believed, that perseverance in the honour that she has meant to shew me, must ultimately be victorious; but, where partiality is not desired, it can only be repaid, by man to woman as by woman to man, from weakness, or vanity. Gratitude is all-powerful in friendship, for friendship may be earned; but love, more wilful, more difficult, more capricious,—love must be inspired, or must be caught. When Elinor, who possesses many of the finest qualities of the mind, sees the fallacy of her new system; when she finds how vainly she would tread down the barriers of custom and experience, raised by the wisdom of foresight, and established, after trial, for public utility; she will return to the habits of society and common life, as one awakening from a dream in which she has acted some strange and improbable part.—'

A sound quick, but light, of feet here interrupted the *tête à tête*, followed by the words, 'My sister! my sister!' and, in less than a minute, Lady Aurora was in the arms of Juliet. 'Ah!' she cried, 'You are not, then, gone! dear—cruel sister!—yet you could quit me, and quit me without even a lastadieu!'

'Sweetest, most amiable of sisters!' cried the happy Juliet; 'can you wonder I could not take leave of you, when that leave was, I feared, to sunder us for life? when I thought myself destined to exile, slavery, and misery? Could I dare imagine I was so soon to be restored to you? Could I presume to hope that from anguish so nearly insupportable, I was destined to be elevated,— every way!—to the summit of all I can conceive of terrestrial happiness!'

The grateful Harleigh, at these words, came forward to present himself to Lady Aurora; who learnt with enchantment the purposed alliance; not alone from the prospect of permanent happiness which it opened to her sister, but also as a means to overcome all possible opposition, on the part of Lord Denmeath, to a public acknowledgment of relationship.

Juliet, who, in the indulgence of sentiments so long and so imperiously curbed, found a charm nearly as fascinating as that which their avowal communicated to Harleigh, began now, with blushing animation, to recount to her delightedly listening Aurora, the various events, the unceasing obligations, which had formed and fixed her attachment.

A tale which, like this, had equal attraction to the speaker and to the hearers, had little chance to be brief: it was not, therefore, far advanced, when they were joined by Lord Melbury; who, gathering from Lady Aurora the situation of affairs, bounded, wild as a young colt, with joy.

The minutes, now, were lengthening unconsciously to hours, when the various narratives and congratulations were interrupted by a loud 'Halloo!' followed by the appearance of the old sailor.

'Please your honours,' said the worthy tar, 'master begins to be afeard you've as good as forgot him: he's been walking upon the beach, alongside the old French parson, till one foot is plaguely put to it to wag afore t'other. Howsomever, he'd scorn to give up to a Frenchman, to the longest day he has to live; more especialsome to a parson; you may take Jack's word for that!'

The happy party now hastened to the strand; but there perceived neither the Bishop nor the Admiral. The sailor, slily grinning at their surprize, told them, with a merry nod, and a significant leer, that he would shew them a sight that would make them stare amain; which was no other than an honest Englishman, sitting, cheek by jowl, beside a Frenchman; as lovingly as if they were both a couple of Christians, coming off the same shore.

He then led them to a bathing-machine; in which the Admiral was civilly, though with great perplexity, labouring to hold discourse with the Bishop.

The impatient Harleigh besought Lord Melbury to be his agent, with the guardian and the uncle of his lovely sister. Lord Melbury joyfully complied. The affair, however momentous, was neither long nor difficult to arrange. The Bishop felt an implicit trust in the known judgment and tried discretion of his ward; and the Admiral held that a female, as the weaker vessel, could never properly, nor even honourably, make the voyage of life, but under the safe convoy of a good husband.

Harleigh, therefore, was speedily summoned into the machine; his proposals were so munificent, that they were applauded rather than approved; and, all descending to the beach, the Bishop took one hand, and the Admiral another, of the blushing Juliet, to present, with tenderest blessings, to the happy, indescribably happy Harleigh.

Juliet, then, had the unspeakable delight of presenting her brother and her sister to her uncle, and to the Bishop. The Admiral, nevertheless, could not resist taking his niece apart, to tell her, that, if he had but had an insight into her being in such a hurry for a husband, he should have made free to speak a good word for a young sea-captain of his acquaintance; a lad for whom he had a great goust, and who would be sure to make his way to the very top; since, already, he had had the luck, while bravely fighting, in two different engagements, to see his two senior officers drop by his side: by which means he had arrived at his promotion of first lieutenant, and of captain. And if, which was likely enough, God willing, he should meet with such another good turn in a third future engagement, he bid fair for being a Commodore in the prime of his days. 'And then, my dear,' he continued, 'when he had been upon a long distant station; or when contrary winds, or the enemy, had stopt his letters, so that you could not guess whether the poor lad were alive or dead; think what would have been your pride to have read, all o' the sudden, news of him in the Gazette!'

This regret, nevertheless, operated not against his affection, nor his beneficence, for, returning with her to the company, he solemnly announced her to be his heiress.

'One thing, however, pertaining to this business,' he cried, 'devilishly works me still, whether I will or no'. That oldish gentlewoman, who was taking upon her to send my Niece Granville before the justice! Who is she, pray? I should not be sorry to know her calling; nor, moreover, what 'tis puts her upon acting in such a sort.'

Lord Melbury and Lady Aurora endeavoured to offer some excuse, saying, that she was a relation of their uncle Denmeath.

'Oh, if that be the case,' cried he, holding his head high up in the air, 'I shall make no scruple to let her a little into my way of thinking! It's a general rule with me, throughout life, to tell people their faults; because why? There are plenty of people to tell them their good qualities; in the proviso they have got any; or, in the t'other case, to vamp up some, out of their own heads, that serve just as well for ground-work to a few compliments; but as to their faults, not a soul will give 'em a hint of one of them. They'll leave them to be 'ticed strait to the devil, sooner than call out Jack Robinson! to save them.'

Lady Aurora was now advancing with a gentle supplication; but, taking off his hat, and making her a low bow, he declined hearing her; saying, 'Though it may rather pass for a hint than a compliment, to come out with the plain truth to a young lady, I must make free to observe, that I never let my complaisance get the upper hand of my sincerity; because why? My sincerity is for myself; 'tis my honour! and whereby I keep my own good opinion; but my complaisance is for my neighbours; serving only to coax over the good opinion of others. For which reason, though I am as glad as another man of a good word, I don't much fancy turning out of my way for it. I hold it, therefore, my bounden duty, to demand a parley with that oldish gentlewoman; and the more so, abundantly, for her being a person of quality; for if she's better born, and better bred than her neighbours, she should be better mannered. For who the devil's the better for her birth and breeding, if they only serve to make her fancy she has a right to be impudent? If we don't take care to drop a word or two of advice, now and then, to persons of that sort, you'll see, before long, they won't let a man sit down in their company, under a lord!'

Then, enquiring her name, he sent his honest sailor to request an audience of her for the uncle of the Honourable Miss Granville; adding, with a significant smile, 'Harkee, my boy! if she says she don't know such a person, tell her, one Admiral Powel will have the honour to introduce him to her! And if she says she does not know Admiral Powel neither, tell her to cast an eye upon the Gazette of the month of September this very day twelve years!'

To tranquillize Lady Aurora, Lord Melbury preceded the sailor to prepare Mrs Howel for the interview; but he did not return, till a summons to the repast was assembling the whole company in the lodging-house. He then related that he had found his uncle Denmeath already arrived, and that he had acquainted both him and Mrs Howel with the situation of affairs.

The Admiral now ordered the dinner to be kept warm, while he whetted, he said, his goust for it; and then sped to the combat; bent upon fighting as valiantly for the parental fortune of his niece with one antagonist, as for what was due to her wounded dignity with the other.

The party, however, was not long separated; Lord Denmeath, confounded by intelligence so easily authenticated, of the duplicate-codicil, protested that he had never designed that the portion should be withheld; and Mrs Howel, stung with rage and shame at this positive discovery of the family, the fortune, and the protection to which the young woman, whom she had used so ignominiously, was entitled, received the reprimands and admonitions of the Admiral in mortified silence.

Nothing, when once 'tis understood, is so quickly settled as business. Lord Denmeath, having given the name of his lawyer, broke up the conference, and quitted Teignmouth; Mrs Howel, confused, offended, and gloomy, was not less eager to be gone; though the Admiral would gladly have detained her, to listen to a few more items of his opinions. Lady Aurora, forced to accompany her uncle, softly whispered Juliet, in an affectionate parting embrace, 'My dearest sister, ere long, will give a new and sweet home to her Aurora!'

This, indeed, was a powerful plea to favour the impatience of Harleigh; a plea far more weighty than one urged by the Admiral; that she would be married without further parleying, lest people should be pleased to take it into their heads, that she had been the real wife of that scoundrel commissary, and was forced, therefore, to go through the ceremony of being his widow.

Called, now, to the kind and splendid repast, the Admiral insisted that Juliet should preside at his hospitable board; where, seated between her revered Bishop and beloved brother, and facing her generous uncle, and the man of her heart, she did the honours of the table to the enchanted strangers, with glowing happiness, though blended with modest confusion.

When the desert was served, the joyous Admiral, filling up a bumper of ale, and rising, said, 'Ladies and gentlemen, I shall now make free to propose two toasts to you: the first, as in duty bound, is to the King and the Royal Navy. I always put them together; because why? I hold our King to be our pilot, without whom we might soon be all aground; and, in like manner, I hold us tars to be the best part of his majesty's ship's company; for though old England, to my seeming, is at the top of the world, if we tars were to play it false, it would soon pop to the bottom. So here goes to the King and the Royal Navy!'

This ceremony past; 'And now, gentlemen and ladies,' he resumed, 'as I mortally hate a secret; having taken frequent note that what ought not to be said is commonly something that ought not to be done; I shall make bold to propose a second bumper, to the happy espousals of the Honourable Miss Granville; who, you are to know, is my niece; with a very honest gentleman, who is at my elbow; and who had the kindness to take a liking to her before he knew that she had a Lord on one side, and, moreover, an Admiral on t'other for her relations; nor yet that she would have been a lady in her own right, if her father had not taken the long journey before her grandfather.'

This toast being gaily drunk by every one, save the blushing Juliet, the Admiral sent out his grinning sailor, with a bottle of port, to repeat it with the postilions.

'Monsieur the Bishop,' continued the Admiral, 'there's one remark which I must beg leave to make, that I hope you won't think unchristian; though I confess it to be not over and above charitable; but I have always, in my heart, owed a grudge to my Lord Granville, though his lordship was my brother-in-law, for bringing up his daughter in foreign parts; whereby he risked the ruin of her morals both in body and soul. Not that I would condemn a dead man, who cannot speak up in his own defence, for I hold nothing to be narrower than that; therefore, Mr Bishop, if you have any thing to offer in his behalf, it will look very well in you, as a parson, to make the most of it: and, moreover, give great satisfaction both to my niece, the Honourable Miss Granville, and to this young Lord, who is her half brother. And I, also, I hope, as a good Christian, shall sincerely take my share thereof.'

'An irresistible, or, rather, an unresisted disposition to procrastinate whatever was painful,' answered the Bishop, in French, 'was the origin and cause of all that you blame. Lord Granville always persuaded himself that the morrow would offer opportunity, or inspire courage, for a confession of his marriage that the day never presented, nor excited; and to avow his daughter while that was concealed, would have been a disgrace indelible to his deserving departed lady. This from year to year, kept Miss Granville abroad. With the most exalted sentiments, the nicest honour, and the quickest feelings, my noble, however irresolute friend, had an unfortunate indecision of character, that made him waste in weighing what should be done, the time and occasion of action. Could he have foreseen the innumerable hardships, the endless distresses, from which neither prudence nor innocence could guard the helpless offspring of an unacknowledged union, he would either, at once and nobly, have conquered his early passion; or courageously have sustained and avowed its object.'

'It must also be considered,' said Harleigh, while tears of filial tenderness rolled down the cheeks of Juliet, and started into the eyes of Lord Melbury, 'that, when my Lord Granville trusted his daughter to a foreign country, his own premature death was not less foreseen, than the political event in which her property and safety, in common with those of the natives, were involved. That event has not operated more wonderfully upon the fate and fortune, than upon the minds and characters of those individuals who have borne in it any share; and who, according to their temperaments and dispositions, have received its new doctrines as lessons, or as warnings. Its undistinguishing admirers, it has emancipated from all rule and order; while its unwilling, yet observant and suffering witnesses, have been formed by it to fortitude, prudence, and philosophy; it has taught them to strengthen the mind with the body; it has animated the exercise of reason, the exertion of the faculties, activity in labour, resignation in endurance, and cheerfulness under every privation; it has formed, my Lord Melbury, in the school of refining adversity, your firm, yet tender sister! it has formed, noble Admiral, in the trials, perils, and hardships of a struggling existence, your courageous, though so gentle niece!—And for me, may I not hope that it has formed—'

He stopt; the penetrated Juliet cast upon him a look that supplicated silence. He obeyed its expression; and her mantling cheek, dimpling with grateful smiles, amply recompensed his forbearance.

'Gentlemen, both,' said the Admiral, 'I return you my hearty thanks for letting me into this insight of the case. And if I were to give you, in return, a little smattering of what passed in my own mind in those days, I can't deny but I should have been tempted, often enough, to out with the whole business, if I had not been afraid of being jeer'd for my pains; a thing for which I had never much taste. Many and many a time I used to muse upon it, and say to myself, My sister was married; honourably married! And I,—for I was but a young man then to what I am now,—a mere boy; and I, says I to myself, am brother-in-law to a lord! Yet I was too proud to publish it of my own accord, because of his being a lord! for, if I had, the whole ship's company, in those days, might have thought me little better than a puppy.'

The repast finished, the pleased and grateful guests separated. Harleigh set off post for London and his lawyer; and the Bishop and Lord Melbury, gladly accepted an invitation from the Admiral to his country-seat near Richmond, of which, with the greatest delight, he proclaimed his niece mistress.

But short, here, was her reign. Harleigh was speedily ready: and his cause, seconded by Lady Aurora and the Admiral, could not be pleaded in vain to Juliet; who, in giving her hand where she had given her whole heart; in partaking the name, the mansion, the fortune, and the fate of Harleigh; bestowed and enjoyed such rare felicity, that all she had endured seemed light, all she had performed appeared easy, and even every woe became dear to her remembrance, that gradually and progressively, though painfully and unsuspectedly, had contributed to so exquisite and heartfelt a union.

Her own happiness thus fixed, her first solicitude was for her guardian and preserver the Bishop; whom, with her sympathizing Harleigh, she attended to the Continent. There she was embraced and blessed by her honoured benefactress, the Marchioness; there, and not vainly, she strove to console her beloved Gabriella; and there, in the elegant society to which she had owed all her early enjoyments, she prevailed upon Harleigh to remain, till it became necessary to return to their home, to present, upon his birth, a new heir to the enchanted Admiral.

A rising family, then, put an end to foreign excursions; but the dearest delight of Harleigh was seeking to assemble around his Juliet her first friends.

Lady Aurora had hardly any other home than that of her almost adored sister, till she was installed in one, with an equal and amiable partner, upon the same day that Lord Melbury obtained the willing hand of the lively, natural, and feeling Lady Barbara Frankland.

Sir Jaspar Herrington, to whom Juliet had such essential obligations, became, now that all false hopes or fanciful wishes were annihilated, her favourite guest. He still saw her with a tenderness which he secretly, though no longer banefully nourished; but transferred to her rapturously attentive children, the histories of his nocturnal intercourse with sylphs, fairies, and the destinies; while, ever awake to the wishes of Juliet, he rescued the simple Flora from impending destruction, by portioning her in marriage with an honest vigilant farmer.

Scarcely less welcome than the whimsical Baronet to Juliet, nor less happy under her roof, was the guileless and benevolent Mr Giles Arbe; who there enjoyed, unbroken by his restless, adroit, and worldly cousin, his innocent serenity.

Juliet sought, too, with her first power, the intuitively virtuous Dame Fairfield; whose incorrigible husband had briefly, with the man of the hut, paid the dread earthly penalty of increased and detected crimes.

Harleigh placed a considerable annuity upon the faithful, excellent Ambroise; to whose care, soon afterwards, he committed the meritorious widow, and her lovely little ones, by a marriage which ensured to them the protection and endearments of a kind husband, and an affectionate father.

Even Mr Tedman, when Harleigh paid him, with high interest, his three half-guineas, was invited to Harleigh Hall; where, with no small pride, he received thanks for the first liberality he had ever prevailed with himself to practise.

No one to whom Juliet had ever owed any good office, was by her forgotten, or by Harleigh neglected. They visited, with gifts and praise, every cottage in which the Wanderer had been harboured; and Harleigh bought of the young wood-cutters, at a high price, their dog Dash; who became his new master's inseparable companion in his garden, fields, and rides.

But Riley, whose spirit of tormenting, springing from bilious ill humour, operated in producing pain and mischief like the most confirmed malevolence; Ireton, whose unmeaning pursuits, futile changes, and careless insolence, were every where productive of disorder, save in his own unfeeling breast; and Selina, who, in presence of a higher or richer acquaintance, ventured not to bestow even a smile upon the person whom, in her closet, she treated, trusted, and caressed as her bosom friend; these, were excluded from the happy Hall, as persons of minds uncongenial to confidence; that basis of peace and cordiality in social intercourse.

But while, for these, simple non-admission was deemed a sufficient mark of disapprobation, the Admiral himself, when apprized of the adventures of his niece, insisted upon being the messenger of positive exile to three ladies, whom he nominated the three Furies; Mrs Howel, Mrs Ireton, and Mrs Maple; that he might give them, he said, a hint, as it behoved a good Christian to do, for their future amendment, of the reasons of their exclusion. All mankind, he affirmed, would behave better, if the good were not as cowardly as the bad are audacious.

To spare at least the pride, though he could not the softer feelings of Elinor, Harleigh thought it right to communicate to her himself, by letter, the news of his marriage. She received it with a consternation that cruelly opened her eyes to the false hopes which, however disclaimed and disowned, had still duped her wishes, and played upon her fancy, with visions that had brought Harleigh, ultimately, to her feet. Despair, with its grimmest horrour, grasped her heart at this self-detection; but pride supported her spirit; and Time, the healer of woe, though the destroyer of life, moderated her passions, in annihilating her expectations; and, when her better-qualities found opportunity for exertion, her excentricities, though always what were most conspicuous in her character, ceased to absorb her whole being. Yet in the anguish of her disappointment, 'Alas! alas!' she cried, 'must Elinor too,—must even Elinor!—like the element to which, with the common herd, she owes, chiefly, her support, find,—with that herd!—her own level?—find that she has strayed from the beaten road, only to discover that all others are pathless!'

Here, and thus felicitously, ended, with the acknowledgement of her name, and her family, the Difficulties of the Wanderer;—a being who had been cast upon herself; a female Robinson Crusoe, as unaided and unprotected, though in the midst of the world, as that imaginary hero in his uninhabited island; and reduced either to sink, through inanition, to nonentity, or to be rescued from famine and death by such resources as she could find, independently, in herself.

How mighty, thus circumstanced, are the DIFFICULTIES with which a FEMALE has to struggle! Her honour always in danger of being assailed, her delicacy of being offended, her strength of being exhausted, and her virtue of being calumniated!

Yet even DIFFICULTIES such as these are not insurmountable, where mental courage, operating through patience, prudence, and principle, supply physical force, combat disappointment, and keep the untamed spirits superiour to failure, and ever alive to hope.